ALREADY GONE

LEONARD PHILLIP WOLFE

Copyright © 2023 by Leonard Phillip Wolfe.

All rights reserved. No part of this book may be reproduced, stored, or transmitted by any means—whether auditory, graphic, mechanical, or electronic—without written permission of both publisher and author, except in the case of brief excerpts used in critical articles and reviews. Unauthorized reproduction of any part of this work is illegal and is punishable by law.

This is a work of fiction. Names, characters, places and incidents either are the product of the author's imagination or are used fictitiously, and any resemblance to any actual persons, living or dead, events, or locales is entirely coincidental.

ISBN: 979-8-88640-971-0 (sc)
ISBN: 979-8-88640-972-7 (hc)
ISBN: 979-8-88640-973-4 (e)

Library of Congress Control Number: 2011962736

Because of the dynamic nature of the Internet, any web addresses or links contained in this book may have changed since publication and may no longer be valid. The views expressed in this work are solely those of the author and do not necessarily reflect the views of the publisher, and the publisher hereby disclaims any responsibility for them.

One Galleria Blvd., Suite 1900, Metairie, LA 70001
1-888-421-2397

CHAPTER 1

Jared looked down at the woman that he was having sex with. She was so beautiful, and so young, he couldn't believe that he was with her. Her long light brunet hair made a bit of a circle on the pillow, like the halo of an angel. Jared leaned his head back in pleasure, and closed his eyes. As he did he could hear her scream out in pleasure, but almost a bit of a painful scream, with a gagging sound. He looked backed down at her. Her skin was colorless, eyes fixed and dilated with petechial hemorrhage, and with a rope burn to her neck.

Jared sat straight up in the bed, looked to the opposite side of the bed, saying. "Damnit, why do I keep dreaming about her?"

Jared is a state police officer. The area that he patrols is interstate fifty seven from mile marker forty four to mile marker ninety six. It was a Saturday afternoon, and Jared was just driving along, going about sixty miles per hour. It was about two years ago, when his wife and ten year old daughter, were driving along this same area. The roads were icy in spots, and there was a strong west wind blowing. Jared's wife Clair was northbound, in their Ford mini van. Clair had just passed a semi carrying a piece of heavy equipment, when her car hit a patch of black ice, and a gust of wind blew the van in front of the truck. The rear corner of the mini van caught the bumper of the truck, spinning it around sideways in front of the truck. The driver hit the breaks, but he too was on the black ice. All he could do was look down at the van with the little girl in it, until they went off of the ice. Then what was bad turned worst. The mini van's tires caught on the dry surface, making the van lay over on its side. After that the truck went up on the van causing everybody to stop.

Jared was sitting at home watching college basketball. It was a great afternoon with a lot of good games on, his teams were winning. He was all alone; nobody could get on to him for being to loud. The doorbell rang. Jared looked out the window, as he went to answer the door. It was a couple of buddies from work, Clayton and Eddy. With a smile on his face Jared opened the door. "Hey come on in, I got some great games on."

As he looked at Clayton and Eddy the smile left his face. "What's going on?" Jared asked Clayton said, "Yeah we need to come in." As he walked through the door, he put his hand on Jared's shoulder. Jared looked at Eddy, whose eyes were already red and teary. He then looked back at Clayton. Tears were already in Jared's eyes before Clayton could say. "Jared there is no easy way to a say this. Clair has been in a wreck."

"How bad is it?"

"Jared they both died at the wreck site."

This was all going through his mind, when he heard over the radio. "Jared can you hear me?"

"Yes, what is it!" After snapping out of his trance, Jared answered back.

The voice came back on. "You have a black Camaro coming up on you. I clocked him doing ninety."

"Ok I got him in my rearview mirror. He looks to be doing about seventy now. Oh he saw me, I'm doing fifty, and he's not catching me." Jared told the other officer.

"That's ok; I'm right on his tail. I'm going to turn on the lights and pull him over", came the reply back on the radio.

Jared pulled over to the side of the road, to wait for the Camaro and the other officer. The car that was being pursued pulled in behind Jared. Jared stepped out of the car, and started walking back to the passenger side of the car. He looked back at the other squad car, to see his friend Eddy step out of the car.

"Are you ok?" Eddy asked.

"Yeah. Why do you ask?"

"It took you a while to answer your radio."

"Oh, I was listening to a game, and didn't hear you." Jared explained. This was a lie because he didn't have a game on the radio.

"Buddy do you know how fast I caught you at. Oh, and if you are going to come up with a lie, try to be original, because I have heard them all. Copy that." Eddy told the man in the black Camaro.

"No I think I have a ticket coming."

"Good answer." Eddy told the man before walking back to his car.

Jared walked back to Eddy's car with him. As he was walking, something in the ditch caught his. He looked down in the ditch. But Eddy said, "Get in the car it's hot out here."

While Eddy was talking to Jared, the whole time He couldn't stop looking in the ditch. "See now there you are, man you have to get over this."

"What. No, no. There is something down in that ditch. I'm starting to think that it is a body."

"What? Where at?" Eddy asked, as he leaned over to look out the window. "Let me get rid of this guy, and then we'll check it out."

Eddy walked over to the Camaro. "Well you can consider this your lucky day. I'm going to give you a verbal warning. But if anybody else catches you speeding in the next thirty days, you're going to be looking at jail time. Now get out of here and keep it under sixty five."

Jared was getting out of the squad car as Eddy was talking to the driver. "Eddy you are so full of shit, jail time." Said Jared as the car drove off.

Eddy walked over next to Jared, who was starting to make his way to the bottom of the ditch. "Yeah well, do you really think that dumb ass knows that. Be careful that you don't disturb the crime seen".

"What the hell. Let me check to make sure she is dead before we rule this a homicide."

"Put your gloves on before you touch any thing." Jared looked back at Eddy as he was being told. "Sorry I guess you know that."

Jared made it down to the body watching every step to make sure not to step on any type of evidence. Upon reaching the body, he pulled out his gloves, put them on, and then turned to show Eddy that he had them on. "Ok smart ass what have you got?' Eddy asked.

"Well dumb ass her head is covered over with some plastic, just a minute." Jared explained, as he carefully peeled back the plastic sheeting. Her skin was colorless, eyes fixed and dilated with petechial hemmorrage, and with a rope burn to her neck. This was a sight that would haunt Jared for a long time.

CHAPTER II

Jared started making his way out of the bed, looking at the clock. "Three o'clock. May be the best night of sleep I've had in a while. Alison Conner, why do you keep haunting me?"

It had been three weeks since the two officers had found the body dumped along the side of the road. Jared hadn't had a good night sleep since that day, not that he had been sleeping any better before. His shift didn't start for another four hours, and all he could do was wonder around the house. He walked down the hall from his bedroom to the living room. The family photos were still on the wall.

He stopped to look at a picture of his daughter Katy. Such a beautiful little girl, why did God take her away at such a young age? Then there was Clair, the only woman that he had ever really loved, and most likely ever will.

At five minutes before seven Jared walked through the doors of the police station. The first person he saw was Clayton. "Whoa, what the hell man you look like shit." Said Clayton as he looked at Jared.

"Good morning to you too." Jared told Clayton, while flipping him off.

"I'm sorry Jared. Do you need to talk to somebody?"

"Like who, you?"

"No. Like a doctor." Clayton said in a sarcastic way. "You remember Dr. Evans."

"Yes. I talked to him after I lost my family. As much good as he done. I could have been talking to Eddy's German shepherd."

Clayton continued on. "Any how what I was about to say is. Dr. Evans has been replaced, by this hot doctor, from I think Texas. You should go see her."

"I don't know. I really don't like spilling my guts out to a stranger."

"Jared you don't like to spill your guts out to anybody. I'm your friend, and I don't know what is going on with you. Just go see her. Like I said she's hot, so go see her for that."

Jared told his supervisor. "I'm going to see the shrink, if that is alright."

Jared's supervisor Richard, another long time friend, waved to him and said. "It's about time."

The counselor that Jared was to go see had her office just a couple of blocks away from the station. Jared decided to walk over to her office, this way it would take a little more time, and just maybe he would change his mind before he got there. Jared stood out front of the office for a few seconds. He looked back at the station, thinking that he didn't need to do this. As he looked back at the station he saw Clayton outside of the station giving him the thumbs up. Jared turned back toward the counselor's office. "Damn I've got to do this now." He said under his breath. As he walked into the building, he thought maybe they will be to busy, and he could walk out, and forget the whole thing.

"Hi my name is Terri, how can I help you?" Asked the receptionist behind the desk.

"Hi Terri. My name is Jared. I saw Dr. Evans a couple of years ago, and I thought I might try to get in to see this new doctor some time."

"Well Kalley should be here at any time, if you don't mind waiting. And it looks as if her morning is open. You can get all the paper work done while you're waiting." Terri said while handing him the forms.

The door to the back rooms opened. In walked a woman with sandy blond hair, just past shoulder length, with slight curls. She was an attractive woman in her mid to upper twenties. As Jared stared at her he thought, even if she doesn't help him, at least she wouldn't be bad to look at. "Hi Terri anything on the books today."

"No, but we have a walk in." Terri said while pointing at Jared.

Kalley looked over at Jared saying. "Well I guess you're my first patient of the day."

Jared stood up, while walking toward the doctor; he placed the clipboard on the receptionist's desk. Terri looked at the papers saying. "I guess we could fill these out later." Jared looked back, smiled, and then walked on with Kalley.

"My name is Dr. Conrad, but you can call me Kalley." The doctor told Jared as they walked into the room. 'We can sit at the table, you can lie on the couch, or we can just sit in a couple of chairs. Just what ever makes you more comfortable, is fine with me."

Jared was thinking that, he would be comfortable with her on the couch with him. "Chairs will be fine." He said while moving toward the chair.

"Okay, you're going to have to give me some background on yourself. Just talk about anything you want to, job, hobbies, and family life, just what ever comes to mind."

Jared thought for a minute, before saying. "Well, I work for the state police, driving up and down the interstate, watching for speeders."

While he was pausing Kalley asked. "I'm detecting a bit of negative sound in your voice."

"Yes I feel like I can do more. You see about a week ago I found a dead body along side the road. I think I should be doing more to solve her murder." He explained while running his fingers through his hair.

"Is that why you're not sleeping?"

"How do you know I'm not sleeping, did Clayton tell you?"

"I don't know who Clayton is. Your face is showing fatigue. Would you like to tell me more about it?" Kalley asked.

Jared stared around the room, while he thought of a way to tell his story. "It's okay, if you're not ready to talk about it yet."

"No it's hard for me to talk about it, because at night I have dreams. Just last night I was dreaming that I was with her." Jared paused for a few seconds.

"How do you mean by, you were with her?"

"In my dream we were having sex, and then I saw her dead. What do you think; do I have a sick mind?" He asked as he looked up at the doctor.

"No, is this the first time that you have come up on a dead body?"

"I've seen my share of fatalities along the roads. It's like she is trying to speak out to me. Now do you think I'm crazy?"

"No, I just think that you believe you have unfinished business with this case. I see you're wearing a wedding ring. What do you tell your wife? Or do you tell your wife about the dreams?"

Jared looked at Kalley saying. "I'm a widow." He then looked back down at the floor.

"I'm sorry. Do you want to talk about it?" She questioned him on the matter.

"It's been almost two years." Jared paused for a few seconds, then took a deep breath, and wiped a tear from the side of his face. "I'm sorry."

"That's okay, take your time."

Jared reached in his back pocket to retrieve his wallet. He then took a picture out of his wallet. While handing it to Kalley he said. "This was my wife Clair, and daughter Katy, they were so beautiful. They had been Christmas shopping in Paducah, when on their way home they hit a slick spot, and the car slid into the path of a semi. The report said that they died instantly. But how instant could it have been. I'm sure that there were a few seconds there, that my wife knew, that she was about to kill our sweet little girl." Tears ran down his face as he talked about his family. "They let me read the police report. That was the worst thing that I could have ever done in my life. Now, I just keep playing the wreck over, and over in my mind."

Kalley stood up, walked over, grabbed a box of tissues, and handed them to Jared. "That's a lot for someone to be carrying around. I know I'm the doctor, but I'm not sure what to tell you."

"Pretty messed up, huh."

"No not really. Did you tell your last counselor all that you just told me?" Kalley asked while taking off her jacket. She could tell already that this man was going to be some work.

"You know, I don't think I did. Of course back then I thought I could handle everything. I didn't need a shrink to try to make me share my feeling."

"So what do you think is different now? Do you fell more at ease talking to me? Or do you think that, you need the help now worse then you did then?"

Jared thought for a few seconds, and then said. "Yeah I think I could be a little more screwed up now." He looked over at Kalley, and then continued. "You're also easy to talk to."

"Look Jared, we have been talking for over an hour. I want to continue to see you, if you would like to continue coming back." Kalley looked over at Jared, Jared nodded his head in approval. "Good why don't you set up an appointment with Terri for tomorrow? I can talk to your supervisor, if you need me to. That way he will allow us the time. And possibly we can get the state of Illinois to pay for your sessions."

Jared thanked the doctor, walked out of the room, and made an appointment for his next visit.

"Will tomorrow at eight be good for you? That way she can rip your heart out again before you go face the bad guys." He looked at Terri in surprise, as she continued to talk. "I've talked to her about some problems too; I know she has this way of pulling out your deepest feelings."

CHAPTER III

Jared walked back over to the station. Standing out front was his friend and coworker Clayton. "How did it go?" Clayton asked, with a concerned look on his face.

"We made plans for a second date."

Clayton looked at his friend smiling, and then he suddenly lost his smile and said. "You mean an appointment for another doctor's visit. She's hot though isn't she?"

Jared smiled at his friend, saying. "I guess so if you're into professional, doctor type, kind of women."

"Jared can you come in here there's someone here that would like to talk to you." Jared's supervisor called out from just inside the door. "Did Kalley help you out any"?

"Yes. I have another appointment for in the morning".

"I know she already called me. I approved for you to see her." Richard said as they were walking inside the office. As they walked Jared noticed a woman in front of them. She was about five foot three inches tall, straight shoulder length dark brown hair and dark brown eyes. He kept looking into her eyes as she approached him. It was like she was drawing him in with her beauty. "Jared this is Kenna Jenkins, she is from the main office."

"It's nice to meet you Jared." Kenna said, while extending her hand out to shake hands with Jared.

Jared looked down at her hand. He thought, even her hand is beautiful, those long dark brown finger, with the finger nails painted dark purple. As he took her hand, she smiled at him. She had a beautiful smile, which showed a hint of sadness in it. "Hi Kenna. It's nice to meet you too."

While Jared was holding her hand, Richard explained. "Miss Jenkins is here to investigate the Conner girl's murder. I told her that you were the one that found her body."

"That was a week ago. Why are they just now sending you in to investigate?" The officer asked while releasing her hand.

"I requested this case. I had heard about it, and it looked to me like some people down here were dragging their feet."

"Oh yeah over a week and not one lead. It's more like there isn't anybody looking for, or even trying to find a lead." Jared explained.

"Would you mind taking me out to the drop sight?" Kenna asked, but already knew the answer; just by the way that Jared had been looking at her.

"Sure." The officer said with a big smile on his face.

As they were driving down the interstate, Kenna turned toward Jared saying. "You said something back at the station. You don't have any idea, that there might be a cover up, do you?"

"Ok, when we called in the body dump, the county prosecutor came out to the sight. If that wasn't odd enough, the sheriff came out with some of his deputies. They took over the area, telling us to leave. When have you known county to have jurisdiction over state? You ask me if I have an idea that, there might be a cover up. Yea, I have a pretty good idea of it." The officer explained.

"Do you know a Brett Harper?"

"Yes. His uncle is Ben Miller, the county prosecutor's. Why do you suspect him?" Jared asked.

Kenna didn't answer, instead she asked. "How much farther do we have to go?"

"It's just one more mile ahead. What do you think you are going to find, it's been over a week?"

"I just want to get a feel of the area where her body was left." Kenna explained, while looking out the window.

Jared started to slow the car, to pull over. "Well this is it. If you look straight down in the ditch, where all the weeds are tromped down, that is where she was lying at." Jared explained, while bring the car to a stop.

Kenna stepped out of the car, and walked over to the edge of the grass. Sarcastically she said. "It looks like the drop site has been well preserved, incase anybody wanted to look it over again."

"Yes this is the way it looked after our counties finest got done."

"So you're saying that the police officers did this." Kenna looked at Jared in disbelieve.

Kenna walked into the area, in a careful manner. Just maybe there would be a small piece of evidence that could help point them in the direction of Alison's murders. "So are you finding any thing down there"?

Kenna looked up at Jared. "No it's been gone over pretty good. I think we need to go see the coroner." the young officer said as she climbed out of the ditch. Kenna sat quietly as they drove along. Jared looked over at her, while she stared out the window. He wondered what she was thinking. Was she deep in thought? Maybe she just didn't like him. Somehow he felt like he needed to break the ice, but maybe he had already talked too much already. Maybe he should just sit back, shut up, and just drive the car. Yeah that is it. All she needed him for is for a chauffer. Besides, he's only a patrolman from down state Illinois and here she is, most likely a high educated woman, coming down here from Springfield, to solve this case that nobody else can.

"So what drew you to this case?"

Kenna looked over at Jared, before saying. "Just a little over a week ago, a picture of this beautiful young girl came over the air, as a missing person." Kenna took a picture out of her bag, handing it to Jared. "Yes she was so beautiful, so young, and so innocent. I wanted her to be alive so bad. Then it came across one day later that she was dead. We were getting progress reports up in Springfield. Well I wouldn't really call it progress, because it didn't look like anybody was doing anything".

Ok, maybe she didn't dislike him. "She was a beautiful girl. Do you have any back ground on her"?

Kenna pulled out a folder, and started to read. "Alison Conner ages eighteen, two months, and one day old. She is from Mesquite, Texas. I guess I should say was. She was a student at Southern Illinois University, Carbondale, as a freshman. She was an employee at Family Video, which was the last place that she was seen at. I think that's another place we need to go. Do you need me to go on?" The young woman asked.

"No. We're here at the coroner's office now."

The two walked in the coroner's office. "Jared what brings you in here," said a heavy set man, probably in his early sixties, with a bald head.

"Berry this is Kenna. She is from the state headquarters in Springfield." Jared told the man in a white coat, standing beside a dead body.

Berry held out his hand, saying. "It's nice to meet you young lady."

Kenna held up her hands. "Nice to meet you to, but if you don't mind, not in here. I kind of have a bit of a handshaking phobia, and in here it is really strong. It's something I inherited from my dad."

"That's ok, I understand. What can I do for you?"

"I would like to see everything that you have on the Alison Conner case." Kenna told the old man.

"I sent the paper work over to the Sheriff's department." Berry explained, with a worried look on his face.

"You shouldn't have. You should have sent them copies, but all of the originals should still be here, or sent to the court house." Kenna had nailed Berry, and he knew it.

"Look Missy, I'm just about a year away from retiring. I didn't want to make any waves. I just did what I was told. I knew it wasn't right."

"You know that this could be an obstruction of justice. Don't you?" Kenna looked at Berry, as he walked over to a filling cabinet, and pulled out a folder. Berry handed the folder to the young officer. "Dallas Mayberry, what do I want with this for?"

"You don't know where this came from. Just take it and go Missy." The coroner told Kenna as she opened the file.

As the two officers left the building, Kenna said. "What the heck? This is the autopsy report on Alison."

"I'm sure Berry just gave them their copies. He knows not to just hand over evidence."

"Ok. Then what is this?" Kenna asked while handing the folder to Jared.

"Yes, this is a copy too. I've seen him do this before, hide files under somebody else's name, to keep someone from finding them. I wonder who he is hiding it from."

Kenna read the report, as they drove back to the headquarters. Jared drove along in silence. He could tell that Kenna wasn't in any kind of a talking mood. It looked like she was taking this case very personal. What was it? Just because she had seen her file as a missing person, and hoping that she would still be alive. There had to be more to it. "When are you going to take me to lunch?" Kenna asked.

"Oh yeah. Ok, maybe we should stop for lunch." Oh yeah. That was real smooth, Jared thought. I bet she really thinks you're a real dumb ass now. "There's a little restaurant up the road that I like to go to. If you don't mind?" Jared asked.

"Oh, a little bit of home cooking." Kenna said with a smile on her face. Jared just looked at her and nodded. Yeah, maybe he was over thinking it too much. Well you know it would be easy to take a young beautiful girl, getting murdered personal. Wow that is one beautiful smile.

After lunch, the two went there separate ways. Jared went back to patrolling his root, on the interstate. Who knows where Kenna went, but it had to be more exciting then what he was doing. The patrolman spent the rest of his shift driving the interstate, and thinking about the young officer. Jared glanced at himself in the mirror. He was thirty five years of age, in good shape, and had all of his hair. Yeah there might be a little bit of gray, but that just came on in the last two years.

CHAPTER IV

Eight o'clock the next morning Jared walked in to Kalley's office. "Good morning. Back for more, are you?" Asked the receptionist.

"Good morning Terri. Yep can't wait to get started. Is she in yet?"

"Yes, I will let her know you're here." Terri said as she stood up, and walked toward the doctor's door. "Kalley, your first appointment is here, are you ready for him?"

"Yes. Send him in."

Jared walked into the office. "How are you today Dr. Conrad?"

"I'm doing well. You're sounding a bit spirited today. So what's up?" The doctor asked. "Ok. Well I slept better last night."

"And what contributed to that?"

Jared squirmed around, looked around the office, before saying. "They sent an officer down from Springfield to investigate the Alison Conner case. I took her around yesterday."

"Somebody is working on the case. Do you think that is making you feel better?" Kalley asked.

"Yeah I'm sure that is it."

Kalley could detect that there was more that the police officer wasn't telling her. He was a lot happier today, and more at ease. "Is there a new woman in your life?" Kalley questioned. Jared looked at the doctor, in surprise, questioning back. "Why do you say that?" "There is, isn't there!" Kalley responded back, with a smile on her face.

Jared thought for a minute, before he blurted out something, that he might regret. "You know I told you that they sent somebody down from Springfield."

"Yes go on."

"Well I can't stop thinking about her. She's in her early twenties, so she is at least ten years younger than I am."

"That isn't really a very wide age span." The doctor looked at Jared, as if he wasn't telling her the whole story. "There's more to it, isn't there?"

"Ok. Well she's black too, but she is very beautiful."

"I take it that you're not to sure about mixed relationships, are you?"

"No, it's not that. I don't have a problem with it, but what if she does. What do I do or say, what do you think about dating an older white guy, that's probably five pay grades lower then you are".

"I think you are over thinking this. Are you two going to be working together anymore?" "I'm not sure. But she is working out of our local station, so I should be seeing her."

"Ok then. You need to just find some command grounds. The Alison Conner case is a command ground. Have you been able to share any thing with her to help out with the case?" Kalley asked.

"Yeah. Ok I have this theory. I can tell you confidential information, right?" Jared wasn't too sure of what he could tell his doctor and what he couldn't. "You can tell me anything. Nothing leaves this office." "Ok I think there is a cover up."

Kalley looked directly at Jared saying. "Wait a minute. You're talking about the murder of a college student. Why are you thinking there might be a cover up?"

"I think that the county prosecutor's nephew did it, and the county is covering it up. That kid has always been trouble, so it wouldn't surprise me anyway. The coroner gave Kenna a report, which I have no idea what is on it, but there was something on it that caught her attention. Come to think of it she asked me about Brett Harper." Jared paused.

"Who is Brett Harper?"

"That is the county prosecutor's nephew. Kenna must have already suspected him".

Kalley thought for a minute, before saying. "If you think this Harper person could have done this murder, maybe you should dig some information up on him. At least that would give you a reason to see Kenna again."

Once Jared finished up with his session, and made another appointment for the next day. He walked back over to the station. When the officer walked through the doors to the station he had one thing in mind. Find Kenna. He found her sitting at a desk on a computer. As he walked over to her, she said. "How was your visit with the shrink?"

"I beg your pardon; it was a session with my therapist." Jared said, with a smile on his face.

Kenna looked up at Jared to make sure that he was making a joke of her comment. "What do you have planned for the day?"

"Probably just cruise around all day. What about you?" He asked.

"I thought that I might find me a local guy to take me around to talk to a few people. Think you might be interested?" Kenna put on her smile, while asking. It was already obvious, that all she has to do is smile at Jared, and she could get what she wanted.

"That sounds tempting. Sure I'll do it, I just have to check with Richard first." Jared said as he walked off to check with his supervisor.

"Jared do you have any idea what Kenna is up to?" Richard asked his officer. "No, why, what do you mean?"

"Just keep an eye on her." Richard explained. What was up with that, Jared thought. Maybe this is going to get good. Maybe she is on to something. Who knows?

"Are we good?" Kenna asked.

"Yes. Where are we going?" Jared asked, while they were walking out to the squad car.

Kenna didn't answer right away. She waited until they were in the car to say anything. "Well, I thought we might go down to the Sheriff's department, and maybe shake things up a bit. How does that sound to you?"

Jared looked over at Kenna. "Just what do you think that we are going to find out, by going in there?"

"What's the matter? Scared?" Kenna said to the officer with a smile on her face.

Jared started the car while looking over at Kenna. There was that smile. The one that could get him to do anything, and right now it was the smile that was telling him, don't be a weenie. "No I'm not scared. In fact I'm ready; let's go talk to the big bad Sheriff."

"That's the spirit. Do you think we will get anything out of them?" "Kenna, what are you expecting?"

"I don't know. You tell me. You're the one that put the idea of a cover up in my head. Just what are you expecting to find out? Besides, are you just the chauffer, or are you in this for a reason?" Ok now she hit a nerve. She wasn't getting any reply back from Jared. "Don't want to talk about it huh?"

"Well yeah, that's kind of between my shrink and me." "Seeing her in your sleep, aren't you?"

Jared turned to face the beautiful officer beside him, and asked. "How do you know?"

"I've heard of it happening to officers before. Since you were the one that found her, you feel obligated to find her killers. Now in a way it kind of haunts you. I don't need to know the details of your dreams, but you are dreaming about her, aren't you?"

"Yes." Jared replied, and then in trying to change the subject, he asked. "Do you have a favorite college basketball team?"

"Yes I'm an Illini fan. How about you? Illini, or are you a Salukis fan?"

"Illini, I just root for the almost hopeless team, not the completely hopeless teams." Jared explained. "My whole family has been big Illinois fans for years."

"So did you play any sports in high school or college level?"

"I played football in high school. I was all the time setting records for rushing, until my senior year. Two games before the end of regular season, I had my knee taken out. I had scouts looking at me, but that ended my career in sports. What about you, did you play any sports?" Jared asked.

"Well in high school I played softball, basketball, volleyball, and ran track." Jared looked over at the young lady saying. "Is that all?"

"Yes. That is the only programs that my school had. I was very athletic in high school." She said.

Jared asked. "Not in college?"

"No I am five foot three inches, so it was hard to make any team. I just worked on self defense classes, to stay in shape during college." Jared looked over at Kenna. Yeah those self defense classes definitely kept her in good shape.

The two arrived at the county police station. When they walked in, the only people that were there were the jailer, and a local drunk. "Is Sheriff Benson around?" Jared asked.

"He is probably over at the coffee shop, Jared. Do you want me to get him for you?" The jailer asked

"Yes Leon, if you don't mind." Jared told the jailer. He looked over at Kenna, who was snooping around, on the desks. "Think you might find something lying out, do you?" "You never know. This is interesting. It's a file on me. What do you think of that?"

Jared looked at the file saying. "Only been here for two days, and they are already checking up on you. Must be seeing what your credentials are."

Kenna looked over at the fellow officer, with a smirk on her face. "Yeah whatever. They're just seeing what they are up against." She said while going through the file.

"Paranoid are you?"

"No just cautious. There isn't much here anyway." Kenna said as she placed the folder back on the desk. She gave Jared a quick little smile. Okay what did that mean? Does she have a secret past, or was she just playing with him.

"Jimmy's on his way over. Can I get you coffee or anything, while you wait?" Leon asked.

"No we're good." Jared said, as he looked over at his partner, who was shaking her head no.

"So how have you and the family been?"

"I have been good. Becky though, she has the shingles again."

Now that Jared had the jailer distracted, this was a good chance to snoop around again. At the Sheriff's desk she found a locked draw. Jared listened to the jailers boring stories about his wife's shingles, as he watched Kenna take two paperclips, and bend them around. No she wasn't going to, was she. Oh hell yeah. She smiled at Jared, picked the lock, and then opened the draw. With his back toward the young lady, Leon started to turn around, when he heard the draw open. "Did you do any good deer hunting last year?" The nervous officer asked Leon.

That was all it took to turn Leon's attention away form Kenna. On that note he had to freshen up his dip. The man wasn't a very pretty sight anyway. He was in his mid sixties, partially bold, and when he had a chew of Skoal in, he left out his teeth. Jared tried to keep an eye on Kenna, listen to Leon, and dodge tobacco particles. They heard a car door shut, outside of the building. "I bet that's Jimmy now." The jailer said.

Jared and Leon looked toward the door, to see James Benson walk threw the doors. Jared looked back at Kenna, who was just sitting at the desk, like nothing had happened. "Hey Jimmy." The jailer said.

"Leon. Jared. And who is this, sitting at my desk?" The sheriff asked, as he looked at Kenna, with a pissed look on his face.

"Oh excuse me. Is this your desk?" Kenna asked, while she was getting up out of the chair. "I am down here investigating the murder of a young college student, Alison Conner."

"I know of this Conner girl. But I don't think anyone has ruled it as a murder." The over weight sheriff said, while dropping into his office chair.

Kenna glared at James for a few seconds, before saying. "So what are you thinking, accidental death, or maybe suicide, and just happened to end up in a road side ditch?"

Kenna could see the sheriff's face getting red. "Look young lady. You're in southern Illinois right now. You need to watch your step."

Kenna cut him off. "Or what? Come on give me the or else." It started to look like she was pushing buttons now, and she wasn't backing down.

"What do you want to know?' Sheriff Benson said with a little smile on his face.

"There we go, there's that southern Illinois hospitality that I was expecting." Kenna said while, smiling back at James.

"I sure could go for one of those McDonalds' Mochas. What about you miss? Jared I'm sure you would like one. Leon here's some money. Why don't you go down to McDonalds and pick us up some of those coffees." James told the jailer. As Leon left Jared wondered what was getting ready to go on. Was he getting rid of Leon so he could kill them off, had Kenna pushed him too far? "Okay. Leon likes to talk too much. First of all, I wouldn't keep anything in that draw that you picked."

"Yeah I couldn't get it locked back. So what are you going to tell me? You brought me all the way down here for something."

Jared looked at the two in confusion before saying. "You two know each other."

"No not exactly." James said, and then explained. "Alison came up missing three weeks ago and was then found dead two weeks later. And I'm not saying that she had been dead for a while, either. So where was she at for almost two weeks? There is some twisted shit going on down here."

"So how did you get Kenna involved? And what was with that little show earlier?"

"Leon. He's not as stupid as he looks. And I don't know who he might talk to. What has Jared filled you in on about our county so far?" James asked, while directing his attention toward Kenna.

"Well he's brought up a couple of names to me. And what is with that crime seen? You people brutalized it."

"Yeah that was our fine county prosecutor, Ben Miller. That wouldn't be one of the names that Jared dropped on you, would it?" James asked, the young lady, while he took a folder out of his desk draw, and handed it to her.

"Yes him and his nephew, Brett Harper. So your thinking that they had something to do with it, do you?" She said, as she was looking into the folder. "Yeah I have this autopsy report." Kenna said while handing it back to James.

"Been to see Barry already, have you?"

"Yes I have, and he was quite helpful too. So you trust him?" Kenna asked James, who had nodded yes back at her. "I didn't know if Jared was the only one that I could trust down here or not."

"Barry is always thorough, when it comes to his autopsies. Ben kept rushing him, trying to get him to skip over things. I'm pretty sure that his nephew was involved. I mean, come on, why else would he even be involved in the case." James reached under a desk draw, pulled out a disk, and then handed it to Kenna. "This is the video from the store where Alison worked. The last place and time that she was seen. Pocket that, and view it somewhere else."

Kenna pocketed the disk saying. "Thank you. Do you want me to keep you posted?"

"No, just get the bastards." The sheriff told her as they were walking out the door.

The two walked out the door, and met Leon, as he came back from McDonalds. "Leaving, don't forget your coffee."

"Thank you." Jared said, while taking the drinks from the old man, then handed one to Kenna. As they sat down in the car, Jared said to Kenna. "I think you owe me an explanation."

"About what?"

"James said that he sent for you. And what was with you picking the lock to his draw?" Jared asked then took a drink from his mocha.

"Okay. Well like I told you, I received a notice about Alison. Well apparently, it must have come from James. That I just found out."

"But why you? Why did he send it to you?" Jared asked her, and then took another drink from his coffee.

"That's my job missing persons. And as for picking the lock on the draw. You might have noticed, I'm a bit of a snoop, so a locked draw just kind of entices me. Besides it's always good to keep the skills sharp." Kenna explained, while taking a lap top out of a bag that was in the back seat.

Jared took a drink from his mocha. "You're carrying a DVD player."

"No. It's a lap top. Let's see what is on this disk."

"Your coffee is getting cold." Jared said.

"I don't do coffee. Besides, Leon probably slobbered tobacco juice on it."

Jared turned toward Kenna, set his coffee down in the cup holder, saying. "Oh on, you didn't just say that, did you? I was just enjoying my mocha."

Kenna gave Jared a little smile, as she then put the disk in the computer. The time on the recording showed eleven o'clock, just about closing time. At the checkout counter Kenna could see Alison, and another worker. On the other side of the counter was a young man of about twenty. Kenna paused the recording, held it over to where Jared could see it, while saying. "Does this look like anybody familiar to you?"

"Yes. That's Brett Harper. So are we going to go talk to him?" Jared asked, as he started the car.

"No not yet. I want to go to the Family Video store where Alison worked at, first." The young lady said, then went back to watching the recording. On the way to the video store, the two rode along in silence. Kenna watched the recording over and over, before saying. "What did he just do? Okay stop the car. You have to see this."

Jared pulled the car over to the side of the road, and then took the lap top from Kenna. "Okay. What am I looking at?"

Kenna leaned over close to Jared, almost putting her head on his shoulder. She then placed her finger on the mouse pad, to make the video start playing. Jared was just a little distracted, and didn't really see what she had seen on the video. "I didn't get it. What did you see?"

"Okay, I'll play it again. Now this time try to pay attention." Kenna said as she ran the recording back. Okay this time he had to focus, which was hard to do, with her lying on him. All he could think about was the smell of her hair, and if he turned slightly to his right, their lips would meet. "Alright now watch carefully."

"He dropped something in her drink, didn't he?"

"That's what I'm thinking. If you watch carefully you will see Alison drink from her soda, then later she starts to act groggy. He drugged her, then waited outside, and kidnapped her." Kenna explained, and then took her computer back.

Jared pulled back on the road, and then asked. "And are we still going to the video store?"

"Yeah, but first I want to go see Barry. I didn't see a toxicology report." Kenna then put the lap top away, and took out the autopsy report. "Do you think maybe he missed it, or left it out on purpose?"

"I don't know. I wouldn't think he would leave out information on purpose. But James said that he is pretty thorough." Jared explained, or gave his best. At least wise that's probably what Kenna was thinking. Moments later they arrived at the County Coroner's office.

"Back again today are you." Barry said.

"Yes, can't get enough of this place." Kenna said, with a smile on her face. "Did you do a toxicology test on Alison?"

Barry was looking a bit nervous. "You know I did."

Kenna waited for the rest of his answer, before saying. "Okay, did you find anything?"

"You know I did." Okay what's going on, why is he being so short on his answers.

"Well are you going to tell me, or are we going to keep playing this game?" Kenna asked.

Now she was starting to get pissed.

"Look I am close to retirement, and I would like to live to retire, and just live in my little cabin down at the lake, and just do some fishing. You're a young pretty girl. Why don't you just let this go? And Jared you don't need to get involved in this either." Barry was sweating, and his hands were shaking, while he was talking to the two officers.

"I'm already involved." Kenna said to Barry, and then turned towards Jared saying. "You can leave the room if you want. I wouldn't blame you."

Jared looked back and forth at the two, before saying. "No I think I will stay. It's just me. I don't have any plans for the future, only to see justice come to Alison."

Barry dug out a report, and handed it to Kenna. Kenna looked down at the folder that had the name Rex Walter written on the front. She then opened the folder, read the contents and folded it shut saying. "Rohypnol. That is what I had expected. You made it sound like we were going up against the mob, by knowing this information."

"You know how it got in her system, and by whom, or you wouldn't have asked. And yes you probably are going to go up against the mob. There's a lot of that crap floating around this area, and I have a good guess on how it is getting in. If you bring Alison's murder to justice, you're going to have to go up against a drug ring. I'm not too sure that you two want to do that. It would probably be better if some things just disappeared. You know this might be a good day to go fishing." Barry grabbed his coat, and headed for the door. "Now if you two will excuse me, I'm taking the rest of the day off. Think about what I told you, and have a good day.

The two stood outside of Jared's car watching Barry drive away. "Did you know anything about this local drug ring?" Kenna asked.

"I have heard talk of one, but I didn't ever know how big it was, or who was in it."

"It doesn't matter." Kenna said, while she was getting in the car. "We're only after Alison's murderer anyways."

"Oh yeah, and if we get tangled up with a drug ring no problem then huh." Jared said, as he sat down in the car, and started the engine.

Kenna looked over at Jared, with a big smile on her face. "What's the matter, not scared are you?"

"No. Well yeah, but if you will protect me I will be ok." Jared said while smiling back at her. He was making a little joke of it, but honestly he really was in good hands. Kenna might only be five foot three inches tall, but in her self defense class there isn't anyone that she couldn't whip. Besides all of the sports that she was in, during her younger days, she was also in gymnastics. And not to mention, besides being able to beat you in hand to hand, she is deadly with any kind of gun.

"I know you were making a joke, when you said that I could protect you, but you weren't to far from the truth. You ever do any cowboy shooting?" The beautiful young lady asked Jared, with an even bigger smile on her face.

"No, why do you ask?"

"Being from southern Illinois, I thought you might be into that. I like participating in it. It keeps you sharp." Kenna explained.

"And you are telling me this, why?"

"I'm not afraid of these guys. I guess I am just like my dad. He always said that he was only afraid of one person in his life, my mom, and she is only four foot ten and a half." Kenna said.

CHAPTER V

The two rode along in silence for a little while, before Jared asked. "We're on our way to family video, right?"

"Yes."

At family video they found the manager there, Jordan Lane. Jordan had just graduated from Southern Illinois, with a business degree. He came from a small town in Clay County, and he worked his way through college. To Kenna this didn't make him any less of a suspect. "Hi, what can I do for you?" He asked.

"Hi, my name is Kenna Jenkins. I am with the Illinois State Police. I would like to talk to you about Alison Conner." Kenna said.

"Yeah, that's too bad, what happened to her. She was such a sweet little girl. What do you want to know?" Jordan asked.

Kenna, who is always on the defense replies back. "We believe that she was murdered, and I suspect everybody, so tell me why I shouldn't suspect you?"

"Whoa, wait a minute. I have an alibi if that is what you are talking about." While taking a step back, and putting his hands up, Jordan said.

"So you know when she was murdered, do you?"

The six foot three inch man lend forward, putting his hands on the counter, looking down at the young lady, and said. "No, I don't know when she was murdered, but I know when she became missing. And no I wouldn't ever hurt her. I want the bastards to pay too."

Kenna put her hands on the counter, and leaned back toward Jordan saying. "Okay then tell me what you know."

Jordan straightened back up with a surprise on his face. "Okay, there is something going on in this place. I can't prove it, and I don't really know who to trust telling this to. I think that there's drug dealing going on during the evenings here."

"I don't really care about that, I just want to know about Alison."

"That's what I am trying to tell you. I think Alison saw something, and that was what got her killed. Did you happen to see the surveillance video?" Jordan asked.

"Yes I did, and I didn't see anything on there that told me who killed her. Did you?"

"I saw Brett Harper was in the store, and I believe that he has been selling drugs in the store." Jordan explained to Kenna.

"Let me get this straight. You're the manager of this store, you suspect someone of selling drugs in your store, and you do nothing." Kenna grilled Jordan.

"No it's not like that at all. I already have one battery charge on me for throwing him out of my store, once." Jordan then leaned forward on the counter saying. "So what was I supposed to do?"

Kenna stepped back, looked over at Jared, back at Jordan, then with a calm voice, Kenna said. "Okay, tell me what you know about Brett Harper. And there was another person working in the store that night. What about her?"

"Sharon Davis. Her husband Mike is a city cop. They are alright." Jordan said.

"What makes you think that they are alright? Is it just because he is a cop, or what?" Kenna asked.

"The night that I was arrested for throwing Brett out of the store he was the officer on the seen. I'm sure he had to make an arrest, but he was cool about it." Jordan explained.

Kenna turned toward the door to leave. "I think we need to go talk to the Davis's." She told Jared.

"Thank you Jordan you have been very helpful." Jared said to the boy, before saying to Kenna. "Don't you think we need to go talk to Brett?"

"You seem to have it out for Brett, don't you?"

"I just think he is the one that did it." Jared said while opening the door to go out of the store. "Don't you?"

"Yes I think that he is a strong candidate, but we'll get to him in do time. For now I would like to see what Mr. and Mrs. Davis have to say." Kenna explained while getting into the car. "I want to watch this boy for a minute before we go."

Jared looked over at Kenna, and asked. "You don't still suspect him do you?"

"Yes I still suspect him. I still suspect you too. I don't let my guard down around anybody, at any time, so just get used to it. There is something dirty going on down here, and I don't trust anybody." Kenna said, and then just watched the young man put away movies, and go through receipt. "Ok this is boring. He hasn't even as much as looked to see if we had left yet.

"Ok let's go see the Davis's then." Jared asked, while he started the car.

Mike Davis and his wife Sharon just lived across town. Mike was about forty years of age; his wife was just in her early thirties. Sharon was his second wife. Mike was on the drug tack force, and was logging in quite a few hours. His wife Becky grew tired of the cop's life, and ended up having an affair with their son's little league coach, Tom. The two split up after Mike beat the crap out of Tom. Mike could have lost his job, but Tom never pressed charges, because he didn't want his wife to find out about the affair.

Jared pulled the car into a driveway. "It looks like they are both at home." He said as he turned off, and started to exit the car. "Ok how are we going to play this out, this time?"

"What are you talking about? Role playing, is that what you mean?" Kenna asked sarcastically.

Jared pointed at himself saying. "Bad cop." Then pointed at Kenna saying. "Good cop."

Kenna looked at Jared, shook her head, and then said. "Where did you get your police training from, Starsky and Hutch?" Jared just looked at his partner, with a puzzled look on his face. "You just stand back, and let me do the talking." The two officers walked up to the door. Kenna stepped off to the hinge side of the door, and then pointed at the door, for Jared to knock on it.

Mike, a big man, came to the door, opened it up, and then said, while looking at Jared. "What can I do for you, Jared?"

Before he could say anything, Kenna stepped forward saying. "My name is Kenna Jenkins; I'm from the Illinois state police, out of Springfield. I would like to talk to your wife, if that is okay, about Alison Conner."

"Yes, come in, please. That was such a tragedy what happened to that girl." Mike said, while showing the two officers into the house. "Sharon there's someone here to see you."

A dark haired woman, in her mid twenties, walked into the room. "Yes how can I help you?" The young attractive woman, with brown eyes and a slender face, asked.

"We're investigating the death of Alison Conner." Kenna explained, as she went into the living room. "You worked with her that night isn't that right?"

"Yes that is correct." Sharon answered Kenna, and then looked over at her husband.

"Did you see anything unusual going on or anyone unusual in the store that night?" Kenna asked the young woman.

Again she looked at her husband before answering. "No, it was a slow night, and I don't think anybody seemed to be unusual."

"What about at closing time. Can you tell me who was in the store?"

"Well I can't tell you every body's name that was in the store." Sharon said with a smirk on her face.

"What about Brett Harper? He was in the store, and you know him." Jared spoke out, with a hint of anger in his voice.

Everyone looked over at Jared before Mike said. "Hey Jared. What are you yelling at my wife for?"

"Because she's lying, that's why." Jared explained.

Mike's face turned red, as he stood up and walked toward Jared in a fast pace. When he came within two steps of Jared, Kenna came to her feet, and swung her left foot into Mike's chest. Mike turned toward Kenna, as to turn his attack to her. Once he turned Kenna threw her left fist into his throat. At the same moment Sharon was starting toward Kenna. Just as quick as she hit Mike she also pulled her forty-five automatic out and pointed it at Sharon, with Mike lying on the floor gasping for air.

Kenna looked over at Sharon saying. "What do you think you are going to do?" Sharon put her hands up and took a step back. Once she did Kenna holstered her gun. "Now can we get back to our nice conversation that we were having."

"My husband is having trouble breathing." Sharon said, as she looked over at her husband.

"He's okay. And your ready to calm down now, aren't you Mike?" Mike nodded back at Kenna. "Jared try not to provoke any one again. Now like I said before, and let's get back to a nice conservation."

"You were asking about Brett Harper. I think I do remember seeing him in there, just about the time that we closed. But he's in there quite often. He likes the movies in the back room, if you know what I mean." She gave Kenna a little smile, as she told her.

Kenna replied back. "Yes, he's a pervert that likes his porn. And nothing strange happened. Brett got his porn; you two closed up, and went your own ways. Is that correct?"

With a bit of hesitation in her voice Sharon answered. "Yes that's pretty much it."

"Okay thank you for your time. I think we will be going now." Kenna then looked over at Jared, as she was getting out of the chair. Jared started to speak, but with the look on Kenna's face he thought it would be better to just shut up and leave. It was a long quiet walk to the car, and once they were in the car. Kenna punched Jared in the front part of his shoulder. "What the hell is the matter with you?"

"Oww, what was that for?"

"You know what it was for. Yelling out and getting everyone pissy. You pull anything like that again, and I'll kick your skinny ass." Lashed out the five foot three inch; maybe hundred and twenty pound woman. She then crossed her arms, and sat in silence. Jared looked over at her, wanting to say something, but was afraid to. It could be because he would just make her madder, or because his shoulder was still hurting. "Well lets go, there is no use sitting here any longer."

Jared started the car, and while backing out of the drive way, he asked Kenna. "Where do you want to go?"

"I don't know just drive." Jared headed out of town. At this point he thought it might be better to just head back to the station. "Where are you going?" Kenna asked.

"I'm going back to the station, then you can go your way, and I will go mine." Jared explained.

Now Kenna runs hot and cold all the time. She can be pissed one minute, then be over it and happy the next minute. "What did I make you mad?"

Jared turned his eyes toward the young lady, sitting beside him, smiling. "You're the one that got pissed at me."

"Oh, I'm sorry. Don't take that personal, I was just blowing off a little steam."

"But she was lying." Jared commented.

Kenna commented back. "Yes, and she continued to lie, after your little incident."

"My incident! You're the one that put her husband on the floor gasping for air, and pulled your gun on her. And you have the nerve to say that I was out of control."

"Yes that was just a little reflex action. You know protective instinct." Kenna explained.

"I didn't need protected. I could have protected my self."

"No. That fat boy would have eaten you up. Now take me somewhere to eat, it's way past lunch time." Jared wanted to respond back to Kenna, but he knew that she was right. He hadn't ever seen anyone with that much speed. Kick, punch, and draw all within about three seconds. That was so hot. He would be turned on by her right now if his shoulder didn't hurt so badly. As he thought about it he reached up, and rubbed his shoulder. "Sorry about that, does it hurt?"

"No. I don't know what you're talking about. My arm was itching." Jared scratched his arm, and then pulled into a Hardees restaurant. "Is this ok?"

"Yes, this is fine. Was you afraid that I would hit you if it wasn't." Kenna said to Jared, with a smile on her face. Jared just ignored her comment, and glared at her for a few seconds.

The two officers sat back in the corner of the restaurant, to where no one would be able to hear them talking. "Where do you want to go after we leave here?" Jared asked.

"Does that mean that you're not dumping me?" Kenna asked with a smile on her face.

"I was just blowing off a little steam. Unless you want me to take you back to the station, and let you go on your own."

"That's ok. You make a good guide." Kenna explained, as she was staring out of the window. "If you're still suspecting Brett Harper, I guess we could go see him."

Jared looked up at the young lady in surprise. "What are you talking about? I thought that he was our prime suspect."

Kenna turned her look toward the fellow officer, saying. "He's your prime suspect. The only thing that I saw was that he drugged Alison's drink."

"Okay. And that isn't anything to go on. And why do you keep staring out of the window?"

"There is a black SUV setting out there. It just pulled in kind of slow, and no one ever got out. It's probably nothing. Being from the city, you just watch those things." Kenna looked back out of the window, before continuing. "I did get one thing from our talk with the Davis's. It didn't say anywhere, anything about any sexual contact. You found her and she was fully clothed, wasn't she?"

"Yes, but she could have been redressed."

"That's true, but she wasn't. And Brett liked his porn, but he didn't touch her. That is why I don't suspect him." Kenna stopped talking, and looked back out of the window for a few seconds, before saying. "Let's go to his house next." Kenna grabbed up her tray of her half eaten lunch, and then asked Jared. "Are you ready to go?"

Jared tried to finish off the last few bites of his lunch. "Yes, but could I refill my drink first?"

Kenna sighed, rolled her eyes, and then with a smile said. "If you think you must." While Jared was getting more soda Kenna stepped outside, in the mid September sun. She looked down the parking lot at the SUV. She could see the silhouettes of two people in the car, but she couldn't tell what they looked like, or even if they were male or female.

"You ready to go." Jared asked as he walked out of the restaurant. As the two officers crossed the parking lot, the SUV backed out of its parking spot, and started moving toward them. Kenna could now see that the people were two young men in their early twenties. She kept walking, while staring in the front window of the car. Jared noticed that she had taken the buckle off of her gun, and had her hand on the handle of the gun, so Jared did the same. The two stood beside their car watching the suspicious SUV slowly drive by, while the two young men stared at them. "I wonder what that was all about."

Kenna replied. "They looked gay. They were probably checking you out. Do you think we should follow them?" As the two sat down in the car, Kenna said. "What are you waiting on; they are going to get away." Jared looked over at the young lady, as he was starting the car. "Jared, I was teasing about the gay part, but they were acting shady. So just kind of get in behind them and see how they act."

"Okay then I wonder what that was all about. They were definitely watching us, weren't they?" Jared asked as he backed out of the parking spot. As they pulled in behind the black car, it sped off. "Well it looks like we have a chase on our hands."

"No we don't. Just call in the license plate number, and see who it was. This isn't the seventies, we have computers now." Kenna said.

Sometimes her little remarks could really piss you off. Jared reach down and picked up the radio mike, and handed it to Kenna, saying. "Here you call it in; I didn't get the license plate number."

Jared thought that he had her, but she quickly took the mike, and went to talking to the dispatch. "This is officer Jenkins requesting a license plate check on license plate number H, as in Henry two zero, five eight nine." Jared was staring at her the whole time. He was probably amazed that she was even able to get the number. "What, you're looking at me funny?"

"You memorized the number. When did you do that?"

The dispatch came back on the radio. "That car is registered to a Brett Harper."

"Okay thank you." As Kenna hung up the mike she told Jared. "Neither one of those guys were Brett".

"I bet now you wish we would have chased them down, don't you?" Jared asked with a smile on his face.

"No. I really don't care who they were. Now we were going to go to Brett Harper's house. And while we are there, you can ask him who was driving his car." Said Kenna. "The address is twelve twenty two Maple, do you know where that is at."

"Yes I do." Jared said, with a puzzled look on his face. "That address sounds familiar for some reason to me." The two drove on to the location.

CHAPTER VI

The house was a fairly nice house. Not one that you would expect a twenty-three year old man to own. Kenna took the lead as they walked up to the house, while Jared lagged behind still thinking of why he had been to this house before. At the front door Kenna rang the bell, while Jared looked in through a big picture window. "There doesn't seem to be any one home."

"No I suppose not." Kenna replies while opening the storm door, and looking down at the lock on the door knob.

"What are you doing? You're not going to pick the lock, are you?" Jared frantically asked.

"No. Someone has already beaten us to it."

Puzzled, Jared looked down at the lock saying. "You can really tell if a lock had been picked."

"No, but that is what you are going to say when they ask us how we got in." Kenna said, before reaching down, and turning the door knob. Once she did the door came open. "Well lookie here, I told you that the lock had already been picked." The young lady walked into the house, then turned back to Jared to ask. "Are you coming?"

"I guess so. This is about as good of a day as any other, to end my career in law enforcement." Jared said while following the fellow officer into the house.

"Hello, is there anybody home?" Kenna yelled out. "I guess not. It looks like the place has been trashed."

"What are we looking for anyway?"

"Nothing, just snooping around." Kenna said with a smile on her face, and then asked. "Do you want to go any farther?"

"The only direction that I want to go is out the door." Came the nervous officer's reply.

Kenna had worked her way between Jared and the door. "Ok, see you outside." She said before darting out of the door, with an evil smile on her face. Jared stood inside, like he had been set up. He started moving toward the door, and once again things were looking familiar to him. Just as he stepped through the door, he heard Kenna say. "Ah oh busted." He looked out into the street to see a black SUV drive by. As the car sped off, away from the officers again, Kenna said. "That's strange. If someone were coming out of my house, I think I would be stopping to see what was going on."

"This is great. If I keep hanging around with you, not only am I going to get kicked of the police force, but I probably wouldn't be able to get a job as a Wal-Mart greeter."

"Oh I'm sorry. I didn't know you had your retirement dreams set so high. Oh look the car is coming back." Kenna said, just as they were in front of the squad car. When the car was almost to them the passenger in the car rolled down the window, and stuck a nine millimeter out of the window. "Get down. Gun!" Kenna screamed out. When Jared ducked behind the car, he looked back up at Kenna, who was standing there with her gun draw, and pointed at the car. While he fumbled for his gun a volley of gun fire went out. Once again the car sped off. Jared popped his head up over the car, to see Kenna standing there. "Damn it, I missed, how about you?"

"Are you crazy? You could have been shot." The young man lashed out, at his fellow officer.

"Do you see any blood on me?" Kenna asked, and then looked down at her body to make sure that she hadn't been shot. "Nope. No blood and no bullet holes. And what about you, did you even get your gun out?"

"No. You told me to get down."

"Yes. Take cover, not stop, drop, and roll under the car." She stood there for a few seconds, while Jared walked around the back of the car, and then started to walk toward Kenna. As he looked toward the front of the car he could see how the bullets had hit all around Kenna without striking her. "Well I wish now that we would have chased them down earlier, because now we have a flat tire and we can't chase them."

"I'm going to have to call this in. Was Brett Harper in the car?"

"How should I know?"

"I don't know how, but you just know these things. So was he?" Jared asked again.

"He wasn't the driver or the shooter." Kenna told Jared, and then looked around. Most people would be shaking by now or at least have cold chills. "I think that we pissed somebody off. You probably shouldn't have gone into the house."

Jared looked up from the phone, which he was trying to dial, to see her smiling at him. "It's always a big joke to you, isn't it? We break into a house. We get shot at, and then you try to make jokes."

"I was just trying to break the tension. I could tell that you were upset, and I was trying to calm you down. I'm sorry."

"Hey I don't have a death wish, but I suppose you're used to being shot at."

Kenna grabbed her shirt, and bra, pulling them up to her neck, exposing the front of her body. "Yes I'm used to being shot at. Go ahead and count them, seven bullet holes." This whole time Jared has been with her he imaged seeing her naked, and now all he could do is stare at the bullet holes. "So what do you expect for me to do cry about it? I'm sorry I'm passed that." She then turned her back to Jared, as she put her clothes back down.

"Hello Richard. We have been shot at."

"Shot at, by who, and where are you, are youns okay?" Jared's supervisor asked.

"Yes, we are okay. We are in Carbondale, at twelve twenty two Maple, and the shooters were in a black two thousand nine Chevy Tahoe. License plate number, what was that again, Kenna?"

"H two zero five eight nine." Kenna replied

"Sir it is H as in Henry two zero five eight nine. It should be easy to spot. It has bullet holes on the right side, and the back right side windows have been shot out." Jared explained.

"I'm going to run the number, and I will send a car to get you two."

"I know who the car belongs to, and we don't think he was in the car. And if it's okay with you, we just need a car, so we can finish our investigation. We have a flat tire." Jared said to his supervisor.

"Are you sure you don't need to come in? You two must be shook up a bit." Richard asked.

"No we will be fine. Just send us a car." Jared looked up at Kenna, who was nodding her head in approval. "So, what?"

Kenna cut him off. "I was in a shoot out. I was hit seven times. I lived. I have done my time with the shrink, and I don't want to talk about it." The two stood in silence for the next thirty minutes, when two squad cars pulled up behind them.

"Damn Jared, you must have pissed somebody off." Eddy said as he and his dog were getting out of the car.

Jared ignored Eddy, and instead called for his dog. "Hey Sarge. Come here boy."

Clayton pulled up behind Eddy, got out of his car, and walked up to the passenger side of the car where the three were hanging out. "Jared could I see you for a minute over here, at my car?" As the two walked over to Clayton's car, he asked Jared. "What is going on? What have you uncovered down here?"

"I don't know. We just stepped out of the house, when this black Tahoe went by."

Clayton cut him off, to ask. "Wait a minute, you were in the house? With whom?"

"There isn't anyone in there."

"Wait a minute. There isn't anyone in there, and you just walked in. You can't do that. That's an unlawful entrée. You could get into some big trouble doing that." Clayton explained.

"I don't think anyone saw us." Jared calmly said, then raised his voice to say. "Well except the two guys that shot at us. And what are they going to say anything. 'Dude saw these two cops walk out of this house that they shouldn't have been in, so we shot at them'." Jared then turned, and walked back to Kenna and Eddy. "Which car are we taking?"

Eddy pointed at the car that he drove up in. "Take mine. Just bring it back in one piece, okay." Eddy said with a smile on his face, but Jared wasn't smiling back. "Or not, that would be okay too."

"Thank you Eddy." Kenna said as they walked over to the car. As they sat down in the car, Kenna told Jared. "You can get out of this any time that you want to."

"Out of what?" Jared asked, as he started the car to leave.

"The investigation, I can go on my own if you want out of it."

Jared stopped at a stop sign, looked over at Kenna saying. "I'm already in this too deep to get out now. So I might as well see it out to the end, unless you are trying to dump me."

Kenna smiled, before saying to Jared. "No. I think I like having you tag along."

Jared let out a small laugh before saying. "Tagging along, that's a good one. If you want a different tag along, you could always get Sarge."

"That's okay. You smell so much better then he does." Jared looked over at Kenna, who was smiling back at him.

CHAPTER VII

The two drove onto where Alison had been living at. The place was a large house that was probably built back in the early nineteen hundreds, and then turned into apartments, in the late nineties. In order to get to Alison's apartment, you had to go in the front door, which was unlocked.

Once inside, there was a set of stairs, and at the top of the steps were two doors. Kenna didn't hesitate, or even think about which door she was going to. She walked up to the door on the right, and knocked on it. The door opened, and a young woman in her late teens, or early twenties was behind it. She was a cute girl, with long brown hair, with little waves in it. She had dark brown eyes and a slender face, with a dark completion. By looking at her you could tell that she was of Hispanic heritage.

"May I help you?" The young lady asked, with a pretty smile on her face.

"Hi. My name is Kenna Jenkins, I'm with the Illinois State Police, and this is my partner, Jared. We would like to talk to you about Alison Conner. May we come in, please?" Kenna asked, in a polite voice.

"Yes, please do. My name is Katy Gomez. I was Alison's roommate, and best friend. We came up here from Texas together to go to school." Katy said, as tears started to form in her eyes. "I can't believe that she is gone. Our moms were best friends, since they were in kindergarten, and we were friends for life."

"You do know that we are thinking that she was murdered, don't you?" Kenna asked.

"Yes. I have already been questioned by the city police, and the FBI."

Kenna looked over at Jared to say. "FBI. Did you know that they were involved?"

Jared replied. "No that is news to me. But I'm not surprised, seeing how the body dump was along the interstate." While Jared was talking, he was walking around the room. The whole time Kenna was keeping her eye on him.

"Why don't you sit down Jared? Your pacing is getting on my nerves." Kenna told Jared. While he was taking a seat, he noticed a picture of a family. The father was a white man, and the mother, and two children were black.

"Can you tell me the names of the officers that you talked to?" Kenna asked.

"Just the city officer, Mike Davis, Alison used to work with his wife, Sharon. He was with another man, but I didn't get his name." Katy explained.

"What about the FBI agent. Did you get that officers name?" Kenna asked.

"No. I don't remember him telling me his name."

"What sort of questions was he asking?" Kenna asked, and then looked over at Jared, to see his respondence to her questions.

"They were just concerned about whether Alison had said anything about what was going on at the video store. They didn't even ask me anything about Alison." Katy explained, while wiping a tear from her eye.

"There wasn't anyone that would want to hurt her, was there?"

"No. She was a sweet girl, and she always tried to keep her nose out of any kind of trouble. You are going to get whoever was responsible for her death, aren't you?" Katy asked Kenna.

"Yes I am. I'm not leaving until I do." Kenna then looked at Jared saying. "Give her your card. Here's my card. If you think of anything, or just need to talk. Just call me." Kenna put her arms around Katy's neck, and whispered in her ear. "Thank you."

"Here is my card." Jared handed Katy his card, then pointed at the picture that he had been eye balling, asking. "Who is the family in that picture?"

Katy looked over at the picture, and then answered. "I don't know. That is one of Alison's pictures." Katy answered then looked over at Kenna.

"Let's get out of here and leave her alone." Kenna said as she was opening the door. Once they were in the car, Kenna said to Jared. "I'm ready to call it a day."

"Okay. Did we even accomplish anything back there?" Jared asked.

"Yes we did. We need to find what FBI agent talked to Katy, if he really was an FBI agent. I need to talk to Richard, so let's go back to the station. Besides we need to get a better smelling car." Kenna said to Jared.

"I know what you mean. I don't know why Richard lets Eddy carry that dog around with him."

"What are you talking about? Isn't he part of the K-9 unit?" Kenna asked.

"Sarge, oh hell no. He just rides around with Eddy in the car. He doesn't have any special skills. The only way that he would attack anyone, is if they were holding a hamburger." Jared explained. Back at the station, Kenna walked into Richards's office, without knocking, or even inviting herself in. Jared had stayed back. Of course it didn't make any difference, because he wasn't going to be let into the room anyways.

He then heard a voice say to him. "Hey Jared come here." He looked over to see where the voice was coming from, and saw Eddy. "I need to show you something, about your girl friend."

Jared exhaled hard, and then asked. "What is it Eddy?"

"I called a contact of mine up in Springfield, and she told me that Kenna wasn't even on duty.

She is off on personal reasons." Eddy told him.

"Okay what kind of personal reasons?"

"I don't know. She didn't say. Does it make a difference?" Eddy asked.

"It makes about as much difference as you telling me that she is on leave. Why are you telling me this?"

"So, you don't find it odd that she isn't even on active duty, and she is down here performing an investigation?"

Jared looked over at his supervisor's office, and then turned back to Eddy to say. "Did you tell Richard?"

"No I thought that I would tell you first. And maybe you would like to tell him."

"Hey Jared, can you come into my office?" His supervisor asked. Jared walked in to Richard's, shut the door behind him, and sat down. "How are you doing? I'm sure that you are a little shocked, after being shot at."

"Yes, I was a little bit right after it happened, but Kenna calmed me down."

"And how did she do that, just by talking to you?" Richard questioned.

Jared didn't answer. He just looked over at Kenna who then answered the question. "I showed him my tits. It calmed him right down."

Richard turned red, and in a shuddering voice said. "Well I uh. Well I guess that would work. We found the car that the shooters were in. We didn't find them, but there is blood in the car. And we think that it came from the passenger. So Kenna you must have hit him. Kenna you said that the Feds are involved in this case."

"Yes, Katy Gomez said that one talked to her. But that she doesn't remember him telling her his name, and he didn't leave a card." She explained.

"Okay I will check into it. You two take the rest of the day off, and Jared I want you to go see Dr. Conrad, before you come in tomorrow. I will call her and make the appointment, for you."

"Okay. Is my car going to be ready tomorrow? If not, can I have a different one, because I think Eddy needs his back?" While Jared was talking, Kenna left the room. "One more thing, Eddy tells me that a source of his told him that Kenna isn't on active duty."

Richard looked at Jared, with a surprised look on his face. "Oh, I wouldn't take what Eddy's sources had to say too serious, if I were you." He then just smiled at him, as if he was just trying to get Jared to forget about it. "And if you don't mind a few bullet holes, your car will be ready tomorrow."

"Okay thanks, I will see you tomorrow."

After changing into his street clothes, Jared went out to his personal vehicle. A blue GMC Sierra, four wheel drive, lift kit, big tires, and loud exhaust, a perfect red neck truck. Before getting in his truck, he looked around, hoping to see Kenna. Not seeing her he continued to get in his truck, to go home. Jared wasn't one to hang out in a bar, and as far as drinking to forget about his trouble, that wasn't anything that he would do. He would probably just go home, fix himself a frozen dinner, drink a beer, watch some television, and then go to bed, with some hope of getting some sleep.

CHAPTER VIII

"Good morning, how have you been, since we talked last?" Kalley asked of Jared.

"Well I don't really know where to start. Yesterday was quit eventful for me." Kalley sat up to hear the officer better. "I was attacked by a city officer. But know problem Kenna protected me, and whipped him. Then we were shot at, well she mainly was. I just stayed ducked behind the car, while the bullets flew."

"You make it sound like you think you were a coward."

"I don't know. She just stood there and bullets went all around her. I don't know if she thinks that she can't die, or if she doesn't care if she lives or dies." Jared explained to his therapist.

"So, what are your feelings for Kenna like today?" Kalley asked.

"I can't stop thinking about her, and I want to be with her all the time. And I'm afraid that when this case is solved. I'll never see her again." Jared paused, and then continued on talking. "I can't believe that I'm telling you this. And I can't believe that I have such strong feelings for her."

"Are you afraid to tell her how you feel?"

Jared's answer was. "Afraid, hell I'm terrified. What if she doesn't like what I'm saying? She would probably beat the crap out of me, or even kill me. But other than that she's smart, talented, mysterious, and very exciting to be around."

Kalley told him. "Well maybe she is just breaking you out of your old hum drum life, and you're mistaking this for love."

"Yes. I'm sure that is what it is." Jared was saying this only to patronize her. Only he knew the truth. And maybe he liked his hum drum life. Not. Once he finished his session, he walked on over to the station.

"It's about time. We have another stiff." Kenna said to Jared as he walked up to his patrol car.

"Where at?"

"Amazingly in the same place that Alison was dumped."

"It must be a popular spot."

Kenna stopped from getting in the car to say. "Or someone is trying to send us a message. It's Brett Harper." She then proceeded to get into the car. While getting into the car Jared looked over at Kenna, without saying a word. "What? Do you have something to say?"

"No, not really. Just thinking about yesterday, when we were shot at. Why didn't you duck for cover, instead of standing up right, and shooting?" Jared nervously asked.

Kenna looked at Jared, with an almost mad look on her face. "Duck where? I was already along side of the car. I didn't have time to run in front of the car. Besides it is easer to shoot someone in the back, when they are running away from you. Then it is to shoot someone that is facing you, and shooting back. Why do you ask? I suppose you think I have a death wish, don't you?"

Jared was really nervous now. Any answer he gave would probably be wrong, and she would slap the crap out of him. "No I didn't know. That's the first time I have ever been shot at." Jared looked over at Kenna, who was just looking out of the window, not responding to his comment. The two drove on to the body drop sight. When they pulled up to the location, Barry McKnight was just getting out of his car. The two officers walked along side of the coroner, while he walked up to the sight. "Good morning Barry." Jared greeted him.

"Brett Harper, what a shame. Yes it is a good morning." Barry walked on up to the body. The two officers stayed three steps behind, from the body. The body had a sheet of plastic over its head. Berry reaches down and uncovers the head. Looking down at the body, he said. "Yeap, he's dead." He then placed the covering back over the head. "Let's get him out of here. Not sure I want to hang around in this ditch any longer."

"Wait a minute. That's it. Aren't you going to look him over any better then this?" Came a voice from the crowd.

Barry looked over the crowd. Then with a smile on his face he said. "Ben Miller, what a pleasant surprise. What brings you out here?"

"You know what brings me out here. That is my sister's son, and I demand a little more respect." Ben said as he moved closer to the coroner.

Kenna stepped in between Ben and Barry, saying. "You need to stay back. This is considered to be a crime scene."

"Who in the hell do you think you are?"

"I'm from the state police, and you need to step back." Kenna explained.

Ben looked pass the young lady in front of him, to see Barry smiling at him. Barry knew that this arrogant asshole wasn't going to push Kenna around. Ben turned his attention back to the officer that was standing in front of him, to say. "Young lady, I don't think that you have any jurisdiction here." He then put his right hand on her shoulder.

Kenna took her left hand, grabbed his wrist, putting her thumb into his carpal tunnel. She then took her left hand, and grabbed his elbow, pulling down causing him to twist, and go to his knees. "You want to talk jurisdiction. You just had your hand on my jurisdiction. Now I can let you up, and you can just back up like I told you. Or we can go down to the county lock up. It's your choice." She then released Ben.

Ben rolled around on the ground, in order to get to his feet. "I will talk to your supervisor."

"I'm working under Richard Moore right now. Do you want me to give you his number?" Kenna asked. Ben didn't answer. He looked over at her, and then just walked away.

"Not making friends today, are you girl." Barry said to Kenna, and then held out his hand to her. "Why don't you help an old man out of this ditch? Oh good here comes the meat wagon, with the buzzard brothers in side." The ambulance pulled up, and two men exited the vehicle. The man on the passenger side stepped out of the truck, and then slid down the hill laughing.

"Are they drunk?" Kenna asked Barry.

"No just stupid. Come on boys. I would like to get this body out of here before lunch. You might want to step back missy." Barry informed Kenna, then the two stepped back a few steps. "That is Mac, and Melvin Marshal, you know their uncle." Barry didn't explain to her, who their uncle is, he knew she would be able to figure it out on her own. When the two stepped out from behind their rig, Mac spit out a big wad of tobacco spit.

Kenna looked over at Berry to say. "I am betting that Leon Dow is their uncle."

"You nailed it Missy."

The two boys were arguing all the way over to the dead body. Kenna shook her head, and then asked Barry. "They look like they could be the inbred sons of Leon. You don't let them pick up live bodies too do you?"

"No. That is why I call them the buzzard brothers. We just let them transport dead bodies." Barry explained, and then yelled down at the two boys. "Be careful this is a crime scene."

Melvin, the older of the two yelled back up to Barry. "No problem boss." As he was putting the body on the stretcher it rolled off the side.

"What idiots. They could be the inbred sons of Leon's." Barry said to Kenna, and then turned back around in time to see Melvin, who was pushing the stretcher up the hill. Fall face down on the body, with his face in the crotch of the body.

Mac then laughed, and yelled out. "Look he is giving Brett a blow job."

"Would you dumb asses try to be a little more discreet? Now come on, just get that body loaded." The Coroner yelled out at the two.

Kenna turned toward the traffic in order to keep from laughing at the two idiots working to get the body up the ditch bank. Looking at the cars go by she noticed a familiar face in one of the cars passing by. "Jared. Look, there goes the man that was driving the car that had the man that was shooting at us."

"What? Are you sure?" Jared said as he turned to see the car go by. "I didn't get a good look at him."

"Call in the license plate number and see if we get a hit on it." Kenna told Jared.

"I need a license plate check on a plate H as in Henry two one eight nine seven. The plate was on a gray Toyota Four Runner." Jared explained to the dispatcher.

The dispatcher replied back. "That number matches a blue Ford Taurus, and it has been reported stolen. Where was this car spotted at?"

"The car was spotted on interstate fifty seven near mile marker number fifty six going south." "Okay we have an officer in the area. I will notify them to watch for the car." The dispatcher came back to him saying. "Jared, we have a report of a black Tahoe that was left at a coal mine. The description of it, matches the car that was in the drive by shooting yesterday."

"Where is the car at Dottie?" Jared asked.

Dottie replied back. "They are bringing it here to Du Quoin. And Jared they found blood in the front seat. They're looking for a match for the blood."

Jared turned his attention to Kenna. "Well it looks like you got one."

"Come on. The brothers have the body out, now we can look in the ditch for any evidence." Kenna said, as she was walking towards the drop sight. Looking in the drop sight was pointless. Kenna could see right away that the killers were thorough, in not leaving any evidence behind. But of course they weren't the first to look over the scene. "Come on we're wasting our time down here."

"Don't think that anything was left behind by the killers?" Jared asked.

Kenna looked over at Jared to say. "No. I don't think that anything was left behind, by the last people who looked over the crime scene."

"What now? Is there anyone that we need to talk to, about Brett's murder?"

"I could care less about who killed him, but I do think that we could count him out in Alison's murder. We should probably go talk to Barry, and see what he finds out. Oh why don't you call your girl friend Dottie back, and see if they caught our drive by shooting driver." Kenna told Jared, as they walked to the car.

"Yes that is a good idea, and she is not my girl friend. She is on her third marriage now, to a guy that would make the Marshal Brothers look good. So I'm out of her league. Besides that she has six kids, and I don't need the baggage." Jared then picked up the mike to talk to the dispatcher. "Dispatch this is car fifty nine. Do you have follow up on the license plate number that I gave you earlier?"

Dottie came back on the radio. "Eddy Boyer was the car in the area. I will check with him. Eddy do you hear me?"

"Yes this is Eddy, and no that car fitting the description did not pass by me."

Jared asked Eddy. "Where are you at?"

"I am west bound on highway thirteen."

Jared shook his head before saying. "And where were you when I called in the car?"

"I was at the overpass coming out of Marion. That car didn't go east bound, or continue south, so I'm going toward Cardondale to look for it. Over."

Jared Called Dottie back on the Radio. "Did you call anybody else?"

"No, but that is a good idea. All cars in the Carbondale area are on the look out for a grey Toyota Four Runner. How's that Jared?"

Jared picked up the mike, put it back down looked over at Kenna, then picked it back up to say. "That is good Dottie. Now give them the license plate number." Jared put the mike down, and looked over at Kenna. "She has her moments."

Kenna said. "Such a sweet girl. Are you ready to go see Barry now?" Kenna asked' with a big smile on her face. She didn't care much for the morgue. As they were going to the morgue, Jared's phone rang.

"Hello. Oh high Clayton. What's up?"

"Jared I'm coming out of Carbondale. And I didn't meet the car that you called in. Eddy would have had to of seen it." Clayton said.

Jared thought for a few seconds, before responding back to Clayton. "We are going to the coroner's office. Will you get a hold of Eddy and meet us there.'

"Yes I can do that."

Kenna looked over at Jared. "What's going on?"

"Clayton was east bound on thirteen, when the call came in about the Four Runner. He thinks that Eddy was lying about not seeing the car."

"Why would he do that?" Kenna asked.

CHAPTER IX

The four officers arrived at the morgue at the same time. Kenna stepped out of her car, and went in to see Barry. What ever was going on with the other three, she didn't think it concerned her. All she really cared about was finding Alison's killer. Jared asked Eddy. "Where were you when I called in the Four Runner?"

"I told you. I was at the intersection of highway thirteen and interstate fifty seven. Why, do you think that I was lying?" Eddy asked.

"I was going east on highway thirteen, and I didn't meet the Four Runner. So why didn't you see it?" Clayton asked. "And what were you doing anyways?'

"Sarge was taking a crap, so we were down in the ditch when the call came in."

Jared shook his head in discouragement, and then started to walk off. "Well I am sure he is in Kentuckey by now. I need to see what Berry has found out."

Eddy asked. "You're not blaming me for this guy getting away, are you?"

Jared just said no, and then went on into the morgue. Eddy probably would not have seen the car anyways. Most likely it did just keep going south, and by the time he was able to get the call in, it was well past the intersection. Jared walked in and stood beside Kenna, someone that he now considered as a professional, compared to his two friends. "What have you found out?"

Barry answered. "Not a whole lot. Brett was strangled by possibly the same type of rope that was used on Alison. And he was drugged to. I'm going to do a tox screen, but I have a good idea what is going to come back on it."

Kenna looked over at Jared to say. "This is either a coincident, that these two were murdered the same way, and dumped in the same spot. Or someone is trying to send us a message. And I don't believe in coincident. I think we're done here."

As the two walked outside, Kenna asked. "Where are your friends at?"

"I guess they had better things to do. Where to now?"

Kenna replied. "Let's go look at the SUV from the drive by shooting."

"You think that they might be tied in with the murder of Alison?" Jared asked.

"Probably not, but somewhere we have pushed the wrong button. It may not be connected to Alison, but I'm curious as to who these people are." Kenna explained to Jared as they were getting into the car, to head back to the station. Back at the station the two officers walked around the car, looking it over. Jared didn't have a clue of what he was looking at. "One shot was fatal."

Jared looked up, and over at Kenna. "How can you tell?"

"There was foam in this pool of blood."

Jared was still puzzled. "So what is that suppose to mean?" He asked.

Kenna looked over at Jared and asked. "I guess you're not a deer hunter are you?" Jared shook his head no. "On a lung shot air will mix in with the blood in the lungs, causing foam, when they spit out the blood. My dad taught me this while we were blood trailing deer."

"Oh so you're a deer hunter to?" Jared asked.

"Yes, deer and turkey, but I prefer turkey hunting. It's fun blasting those little bastards with a shot gun. Anyways let's go see if forensic found out anything." She explained, before walking off to the station.

Once inside the tiny lab the two officers met up with Jackie Baker, the lab tech. "High Jared, how are you doing?"

"I'm fine Jackie thanks for asking. I would like for you to meet Kenna Jenkins. We are working on the Alison Conner case together." Jared told Jackie, and then turned to face Kenna.

Jackie's eyes lit up, and a big smile came across her face, as she looked over at Kenna. With her hand extended out to shake Kenna's hand she said. "It is so good to met you. Man that was some great shooting. You shot five times. And while under fire I should add, and every shot went inside the car. One even hit the passenger."

Kenna added in. "A lung shot, at that."

Jackie's smile intensified, when Kenna mentioned the lung shot. "You saw the foam in the blood, didn't you?"

"Yes I did. Can you tell me anything else?"

Jackie's smile quickly went away. "I have a hit on the blood in the seat. This man is a very bad man. As a matter of fact, he is on the FBI's most wanted list." Jackie pulled up a picture of the man, on her computer. "Look familiar to you?"

"Yeap, looks like that was the guy that was shooting at me yesterday." Kenna answered.

"How about this guy?"

"Yeah, he was driving the car. Who is he?" Kenna asked.

"Nathan Waters. Mean anything to you?" Jackie asked while looking over at the two officers.

The two shook their heads, no. "Could I get a picture of those two?" Kenna asked.

"This Nathan is from the Atlanta Georgia area. A lot of the bad guys come in from that area. Have you heard about a drug ring in this area?" Jackie didn't give anyone time to answer, she just kept talking. "Of course you have. Everyone has heard of them, well anyways there is talk that these two are pretty much the head of this organization." Jackie looked up from her computer, in the direction of Kenna. "And maybe you knocked out one of the leaders. Here pound it." Jackie stuck out her fist for Kenna to pound, then done the exploding fist. "Girl power. Is there anything else that you need?"

"You didn't tell me the name of this other guy."

"Oops, oh yes. And that would be Jeremy Black. Correction, I should say was Jeremy Black." Jackie then laughed, and let out a little snort. "Oops. Would that be all?"

"No, you have been very helpful, thank you." Kenna turned to Jared to say. "I need to go talk to Richard. After that I'll let you take me out to lunch."

Kenna went off to talk to Richard, leaving Jared behind. He wasn't sure if this was going to be a private meeting or if he should go in with her. Jared stayed about five steps behind. Kenna went inside of the office, with the door held open she turned, and looked back at Jared. "Are you coming?"

"What is this, don't you ever knock? What if I was busy?" Richard asked.

With a bit of sarcasm in her voice, she asked back. "Are you busy?"

With Kenna staring down at him, he humbled himself. "No I'm not, come on in. What can I do for you?"

"Have you talked to your person in the lab Jackie, about the car that was brought in?"

"Yes I have." Richard answered. At that time Kenna placed the pictures on the desk. Richard turned red, and started to look nervous. "I know. I'm aware of the fact that these two were in the car."

"So what is being done to find them?" Kenna asked.

"I have alerted the FBI, and we are checking all medical facilities, for a gun shot victim."

"That's it?"

Richard stood up, and leaned across his desk hoping to get the upper hand on Kenna. "I don't have the man power to send out beating the bushes for these two men. And why, just cause you stirred up a hornets nest. Besides don't you have a murder case to work on?"

Kenna leaned back across the desk, causing Richard to back up. "Yes I do, and maybe I have two murders to work on." Kenna straightened, to let Richard to get at ease. "Who are you talking to at the FBI, and why are we involving them?"

"First of all, I am involving them because we're in a point down here, and these people can cross the state line pretty quick, and out of our jurisdiction. And if you must know the person that I have been talking with at the FBI, is Claudia Beckham." Richard sat back down in his chair, with a smile on his face. "Oh, and don't think that you are going to push her around like you do us."

Kenna stared across the desk at Richard, as she said. "Jared it looks like we are going to go talk to Ms. Claudia Beckham." She continued to stare at Richards until his smile went away.

The two officers turned, walked out the door, and headed to the area FBI headquarters. The two officers rode along in silence. Kenna just looked out of the window, while Jared sat there wondering what she was thinking about, and if there was anything that he could say to break the ice. "Do you think that I am pushy?" Came the question from the passenger's seat.

Holy shit, Jared thought. He could either lie to her, or just say yes and suffer the consequences. "I wouldn't say pushy just maybe a little persuasive."

"And what is the definition of persuasive, pushy?" Kenna glared at her partner, waiting on an answer.

"Oh, okay, maybe so. But just, just a little bit."

"I know. I like getting my way. Are you going to let me starve all day, or are you going to take me to lunch."

"There's a Hardies. How does that sound?"

"Sounds good. I like their chicken strips. Dad always said that kids love there chicken strips. I guess that I never out grew that." After lunch they continued on to the FBI area office. Once they arrived at the office, they met up with Claudia Beckham.

"Please come into my office. As you know my name is Claudia Beckham." Claudia said as she held out her hand to greet the two officers.

"My name is Kenna Jenkins, and this my partner Jared Keppler."

"Hi it's nice to meet you two." Claudia said, as she shook hands with the two officers. "So what can I do for you?"

Kenna spoke up. "We are working on the Alison Conner case. And it seems that you also have someone on the case. And I didn't ever catch the agent's name."

Claudia looked over at Kenna in surprise. "I'm sorry, but there isn't anyone in particular on the case. All that we are doing is following leads, given to us by the local departments."

"One of your agents spoke with Alison's roommate Katy Gomez, but did not give his name or leave a card for her." Kenna explained to the agent.

"I don't know of anyone by the name of Katy Gomez, and my agents always give their name, and leave a card. Whoever talked to this girl wasn't one of my agents."

Kenna looked over at Jared. "We should probable send someone to check on her."

"Okay, I'm on it." Jared said as he took out his phone, and then stepped out of the room. "Eddy can you do me a favor."

"Sure as long as it isn't anything to hard."

"I just need for you to go check on somebody for me." Jared took out his note book, and read of the address to Eddy.

"Okay got it buddy, heading that way right now."

Jared walked back to Claudia's office, thinking about the decision that he had made on sending Eddy to check on Katy. "Okay it's taken care of. I sent Eddy."

Kenna smiled back at Jared in approval. "Here is everything that they have on Nathan, and Jeremy. Looks like we done them a favor by taking out Jeremy. Oh, and we should probably bring Katy into the station, to have her look over some pictures, to find out who was posing as an FBI agent and to protect her."

"You two might consider some protection yourselves. You are up against some pretty rough people." The FBI agent urged.

"I have my protection, right here." Kenna said, while patting her holstered gun.

The two women look over at Jared. He then pointed at Kenna, and said. "She is my protection. She has got me into this mess, so the least she could do is watch over me." Once the two were outside of the office, Jared asked Kenna. "Trust her?"

"Nope, not one bit."

"Where to now?" Jared asked as they sat down in the car.

"I think we need to go back to the station, and see if Katy can identify our FBI imposter. Right now we are at a dead end. The only prime suspect that we had is lying in the morgue. You want to call Eddy, and see if he has picked up Katy yet?"

Jared called Eddy. "Have you arrived at Katy's apartment yet?"

"Copy that buddy. Knocking at her door now." The two officers waited for some responds, while the big blond headed officer knocked on the door. "Katy Gomez."

"Yes, that is right. How can I help you?"

"Jared Keppler sent me to get you. You know Jared, he and Kenna Jenkins were here yesterday." Eddy explained.

"Yes let me get my purse, and I will be right with you."

"Okay got the package, and delivering to the station. Copy that."

"Okay, thanks a lot. We will meet you there." Jared said, hung up the phone, and then drove on to the station. They arrived at the station at the same time as Eddy.

"So what is this all about?" Eddy asked Jared, while Kenna escorted Katy into the station.

"Katy said that the FBI went to visit her. But the area supervisor says that there wasn't any agent that went to talk to her. So we brought her in to look at some pictures, so maybe we can find this guy. What about you, do you have any new information?"

"No, nothing at all. Why, what were you expecting me to know?" Eddy asked.

Jared had started to walk into the station, but turned back, saying. "I don't know, maybe some more information about Kenna from your reliable source."

"Why, you're not going to listen anyways? Tell me what it is about her, you obviously find something fascinating about her." Eddy asked.

"Yes I do. She makes me feel alive for a change. Come on tell me that you're not just a little bet jealous of me. I mean here I am riding round with this young hot chick, busting people for information, getting shot at."

"Whoa." Eddy interrupted. "Getting shot at, you find that exciting."

Jared went on. "Yeah, I believe I do. Oh let's not forget. She smells a whole lot better then your partner." Jared smiled, walked toward the door, then turned back to say. "Copy." Jared walked in on Kenna and Katy, looking over some pictures. "Getting anywhere?"

"Yes, we found our suppose to be FBI agent. It's none other than our man, Nathan Waters." Kenna answered. "We need to get Katy some protection, so what do you think, do we call Claudia, or take care of this with state police officers?"

"Well I have a three bedroom house, she could stay with me."

Kenna smiled, and said. "Three bedrooms, sounds great we'll move in tonight. Now I am going to take Katy back to the apartment to get some things, so you might want to go home and get your house ready for two women."

Jared couldn't believe that Kenna agreed to let Katy stay at his house, but he really couldn't believe that Kenna was staying to. "You're staying at my house too?"

"Yes, is that alright with you? I mean think about it. Somebody needs to protect you two. So is that okay."

"No I totally agree. I need to go get the house ready." Jared started to walk away, but then turned back to say. "Oh I need to tell you where I live at."

Kenna said. "That's alright. I already know."

"How do you know where I live?" Jared asked.

"I followed you home yesterday."

With a puzzled look on his face, Jared asked. "Why did you follow me home?"

"So I could find out where you lived." Kenna explained. She could see that Jared was still puzzled. "How else was I going to find out where you lived? Okay and maybe I have a bad habit of stocking people."

Jared seemed to be pleased with her answer.

CHAPTER X

Jared headed for home, while Kenna took Katy to her apartment to get some clothes. Back at his house Jared cleaned and straightened up, dusting, vacuuming, the whole works. Once he was done cleaning, he thought about making dinner. Maybe lasagna or a casserole would be nice. Jared went into the kitchen, to start cooking. He heard a car out in his drive way. He looked out to see Kenna and Katy getting out of Kenna's white Camaro. Jared went back to cooking. He knew not to bother with going to the door, because Kenna would just let herself in anyways. And if the door was locked, she would pick the lock, or just kick it in.

"It sure smells good in here. Are you cooking us dinner?" Kenna asked.

"Yeah, just throwing together a casserole. I have a bottle of wine in the fridge cooling, or if you would like to have a beer there's some of those in there too."

"A beer sounds good to me. What about you Katy?" Kenna asked.

"Yes I do believe I could use one, after today." Katy answered.

"Okay three beers then." Jared went after the beers. Kenna drank half of her beer down in one drink. "Oh shit the pan is boiling over." Jared said as he rushed to the stove. As soon as he moved a shot came through the window, just missing Jared. "What the hell?"

Kenna yelled out. "Katy, Jared gets down. Jared where did that shot come from?"

"I don't know, but it came threw the kitchen window." He explained.

"Quick fire off a few rounds through the window so I can see where the shooter is at." Jared quickly shot three shots out the window, then ducked back down. Once he did the shooter shot back one shot. "Got him. He's about two hundred yards out in some weeds. We're not going to be able to get him with hand guns at that distance, do you have a rifle?"

"Yes, but all it is, is a seventeen. Will that do you any good?" Jared asked.

"Yes as long as you can hit a pie plate at two hundred yards with it."

"Yeah sure that shouldn't be a problem." Jared said, and then started to make a move toward his bedroom.

"Wait." Kenna yelled out, right before another bullet came through the living room window. "Let me draw cover for you first."

Jared looked up at Kenna from off the floor, and said. "Tell me when."

"Now." Kenna yelled out, as she fired off ten rounds out of her forty five automatic. She then dropped back down behind the couch that she was hiding behind. Jared returned with the seventeen rifle. "Toss it to me then get ready to fire off a few rounds through the kitchen window again."

Kenna sat up on the couch beside the window. Jared tossed her the rifle, and she started to swing into position, when Jared said. "Here are the bullets."

Kenna slid off the couch onto the floor, and then said. "Jared, you gave me an empty gun." Jared tossed Kenna the box of bullets. She took the empty clip out of the gun. While she was loading the clip, she stared Jared down. "Here we are in the middle of a gun fight, and you hand me a gun that isn't even loaded. Now go over to the kitchen window, and get ready to lay down some cover shots for me."

"Sorry." Jared said, as he crawled to the kitchen. About the time that he was into position he heard the click of the magazine going into the rifle, then the action of the bolt.

"Jared do you have an idea of where he is?"

"Yes vaguely." Jared said, as he hid behind the cabinet.

"Okay, good enough. Aim about two feet over his head, and empty your clip, then I will take him out." Kenna said as she readied herself to make the kill shot.

"Wait a minute." Jared looked over at Kenna, but whatever he was about to say suddenly didn't matter. "Okay, ready."

"I won't let him get you." Kenna said to Jared. Those words were comforting to him, so he nodded to her then rose up and started to empty his clip out of the window. After the tenth shot he dropped back down to the floor. He heard the seventeen fire off, and then he heard what sounded like someone splitting a pumpkin.

"There, got him." Kenna said in a calm voice, like this was an everyday routine. "We should probably call this in now." Those words barely came out of Kenna's mouth, when lights started to come down the road, with the sound of sirens. "Katy are you okay."

"Yes." Came the voice of the young lady, from the hallway.

"Okay, just stay there for a little bit longer. Jared how are you doing?" Kenna asked, while she was changing out her empty clip, in her forty-five.

"I'm good, so shot a seventeen before I'm guessing?" Jared asked, and then changed out his empty clip. He wasn't sure of why he was reloading his gun. Maybe because Kenna was.

"Yes. I used to squirrel hunt with one when I was younger. By the way it's shooting two inches high."

"Jared everything alright in there?" Came a voice from outside.

With his gun still in his hand Jared stood up, and walked to the front door. "This is Jared. I'm coming out. I have my gun in my hand, so don't shoot." Jared walked out of the door, and saw that the police officer was Gregg Meyers, a fifteen year veteran on the county police force, and at this point probably the only cop that Jared could trust.

"I have a report of gun shots fired in this area. And I know that you are not practicing here inside the city limits." Gregg said.

Jared walked on out to the squad car. "No I'm not practicing. Shine your spot light over in those weeds." Jared pointed in the direction of the shooter.

"What the hell. Who is that?" Gregg asked as he pulled out his gun and started to walk over in the direction of the shooter. "He looks to be dead." Gregg walked over, and rolled the man over. He had a single gun shot to the bridge nose. "I believe you got him Jared. Who is he?"

"I don't know, but he fired first." Jared stared at the man. Kenna said that his gun was shooting two inches high, so she must have been aiming for his mouth, but that was still a good shot.

"Who is he?" Kenna was standing behind the other two officers.

Jared answered. "We don't know. You were aiming for his mouth."

"Yeah, he was smiling. Is back up coming?"

Gregg answered. "Sheriff Benson is on the way." He then checked the man for a wallet. "No wallet. This is a professional hit isn't it?" Gregg looked at the two officers, waiting on an answer.

"It's starting to look that way." Jared answered.

"What have you two got yourselves into?"

"We're working on the Alison Conner case. And now this is the second time in two days that we have been shot at." Jared explained. At that time two more squad cars came down the road. The first one there was the sheriff, then a state car. It was Richard, Jared's Supervisor.

James stepped out of the car. "So what have we got going on here? Damn, right between the eyes. Who is he?"

Gregg answered. "We don't know, but we're thinking that it was a professional hit."

James turned to Richard, who was walking up on the scene. "We have a dead hit man here. Why is there a hit man in my county?"

"I would guess it's because these two have stepped into some real crap. And I think it's the local drug ring. I know who this man is. He is, or was the brother of Jeremy Black, and if I'm not mistaking he was after revenge." Richard explained, while looking at Kenna.

James asked. "So what are we going to do?"

"Well first of all. We need to get that young girl, which they were supposed to be protecting away from them. Nobody is safe around them now." Richard explained. "Next we need to get a meat wagon in here, to get this man out of here."

"Who's going to watch out for these two?" Gregg asked, while pointing at Jared, and Kenna.

Richard looked over at Gregg. "Why, are you volunteering?"

"Well no, not exactly."

With a little bit of a smile on his face, Richard said. "I was just joking. All we would be doing is putting you in harms way. They are better off if these two alone stick together. Don't you agree Jimmy?"

"Yes I agree, one hundred percent. Kenna is their best protection." James called the coroner. "Hey Barry, you need to send your boys out to Jared's house to pick up a dead one."

"Good guy or bad guy?" Berry asked.

"Definitely a bad guy."

"Okay, I will get the brothers and head out to make the pick up. So Jared is okay then, right?" Barry asked.

"Yeah a bit shaken, but alright." After hanging up the phone, James turned to Richard. "What do you say these two get out of here?"

"That would probably be a good idea. I've already called in some help, so why don't you two go to the hotel for the night. Kenna you already have a room, don't you?" Richard turned his attention to the young lady.

"Yeah we can go back there. I'll just get my stuff." Kenna walked into the house to get her bag.

After she had left Richard pulled Jared to the side. "Are you still okay with teaming up with her? If not, just say the word and I will get you out of this."

"No, I'm willing to see this out. How bad can it get anyways?" Jared asked.

"Jared, I'm at the Super Eight, room number one thirty two. You want me to wait on you?" Kenna asked.

"No, that's okay. I'll meet you there." Jared watched Kenna as she was getting in her car to leave. "So did we rattle the wrong people, or is it just her, do people just normally shoot at her?"

"She showed you the bullet holes. You decide." Jared walked in his house. The gun man only fired off two shots, but there were Forty five cases all over the floor, and broken glass. "This doesn't look to bad." Jared said to himself. He grabbed an overnight bag, and put in socks, underwear, pajama pants. He stopped for a moment, and looked into the bag. "Pajamas. This isn't a sleepover."

"Did you say something to me?" Came a voice from the living room.

Jared turned to see Clayton. "No just talking to myself. What are you doing here?" Jared asked, as he was repacking his bag.

"Richard called me, to come and get Katy. I guess I'm her protection now. What are you going to do?"

Jared walked into the living room. "Kenna has a hotel room; I'm going to stay with her. Any comments"?

Clayton shook his head no. "I'm guessing that this is Katy's bag. Be careful my friend." The two walked out of the house together. They looked across the road to see the Marshal Brothers getting out of their truck. Clayton turned to Jared and said. "The buzzards are here. Don't you want to stick around, and watch the show?"

"Tempting, but no I need to get out of here." Jared said, as he was getting into his truck.

CHAPTER XI

On the way to the motel he called Kenna to see if she wanted anything to eat. Jared walked up to the door, with the food sacks, and his overnight bag in his hands. After looking up at the door to make sure that he had the right door he knocked on it.

Kenna opened the door, and then said. "Good, food I'm starving. See you packed your bag. Did you bring your jammies?"

"No. This is a nice room. Is the state paying for it?"

Kenna looked from her sandwich, which was over half gone. "No. The county is paying for it. You want to watch the door while I take a shower?" Kenna finished off her sandwich, and went in the bathroom to take a shower. In about ten minutes she came back out all clean and redressed. She usually kept her hair straighten, but after showering it had some curl to it. And she hadn't put on any makeup, but it didn't matter she still looked beautiful. "Are you going to shower?"

"Yeah, I believe I will." Jared picked up his bag and went in the bathroom. When he went in the room he found Kenna's downfall. There was her clothes and towel all over the floor. And in the tub lay her wash cloth, empty shampoo bottle, and soap wrapper. Jared is a bit of a clean freak, so after he finished showering, and was dressed. He started picking up after his partner. "Here are your dirty clothes."

"Yeah, sorry I meant to get those. Do you care which side of the bed that you sleep on?" Jared shook his head no to Kenna's question. "Okay, I'll take the side closest to the door." The two officers lay down on the bed to go to sleep. Kenna was out in seconds, but Jared lay there awake. He lay there on his back, with his head turned toward the young lady beside him. He thought of how he wanted to put his arm around her, as he started to drift off to sleep. Suddenly he could feel her on top of him. At first he thought that it might be a dream, but he heard her say. "There's somebody out there."

"Damn it is this going to go on all night." Jared said as they rolled off the bed and on to the floor. As soon as they hit the floor the door was busted open. Whoever it was they just started shooting before they were even into the room. Once there was a break in the shooting Kenna raised up, and fired off one shot, dropping the man.

"Come on lets get out of here." She said, while she was heading for the door. On the dresser was a bag that contained a second hand gun, clips, and bullets. She grabbed it on the way by. "He's not alone." Kenna said, before looking out of the door, and into the hall. Kenna didn't see anyone, so she stepped out into the hall toward the parking lot. When she past by the next door a shot came through the door. Kenna quickly got against the wall about three feet away form the door. "Jared." Kenna called out in a low voice.

"What?" Jared asked, as he peeked out of the door way.

"Shoot at him through the wall in our room. On three. One, two, three." When Jared started shooting, Kenna kicked in the door, with a drop kick, and then landed in a crouching position. She looked in the door to see a man lying on the floor. "I think you got him." Kenna said with a puzzled voice, and then started to walk into the room. Jared came out of the room to follow her, when suddenly Kenna saw movement in the room. "Jared get back." As soon a Kenna warned

Jared, she saw a gun come out from behind the wall. She dove back into the hall right before a shot went off. Jared turned into the room, and fired off three shots, hitting the gunman.

"Okay, now I got him." Jared looked down at the young lady on the floor. "Now what?"

Kenna stood up. "I don't know. Go make sure that he is dead and alone, maybe." Jared stood there looking at Kenna. "What? You want me to do it? Fine keep a look out." From the doorway she could see the man lying on the floor. She already knew that he was dead. "I can't believe this shit. I come down here to solve one crime, and here I am getting into gun fights, with god knows who. Okay, he's dead, let's get out of here." They walked down the hall to the parking lot. Once they were at the door Kenna asked Jared. "Where are you parked at?"

"Why, are we taking my truck?"

"This probably isn't over with yet, and I'm not getting my Camaro shot up."

"My truck is over here." Jared pointed at his truck, and the two of them walked out of the building. "There's a police car coming should we wait?"

"No, we still need to get out of here." She no sooner said those words, when a man popped up from behind a car, and started shooting. Kenna raised her gun to shoot, but Jared grabbed her and took her down beside a car. "What in the hell are you doing?"

"I'm trying to keep us from getting shot."

"I was trying to keep us from getting shot. I had my sights on him." Kenna lie on the ground looking under the cars. "Well hero; shoot at him or something." Jared rose up slightly, and fired off two shots.

"I'm empty." He said as he looked down at Kenna, who was still belly down, looking under the cars. As she was watching under the car she saw two legs, and fired off a single shot, hitting his ankle.

"Come on, he's down." Kenna stood up and ran behind the cars, to find the man sitting on the ground, holding his ankle. "Don't even move, or the next one's going in the back of your head." Jared came around the front of the cars, with his empty gun in his hand. "Jared load your gun back up."

"I can't. I don't have anymore bullets, there in the truck."

"In the truck. You only took one clip into the room with you?" She asked, as she lowered her weapon down.

"Well yes, I wasn't really expecting to be in another gun fight. Will you give me some of yours?"

"No. Take his gun. How many of youns are there?" Kenna asked the wounded man.

"I'm not talking." Came his reply back.

"Well I guess we don't need you any longer then. Go ahead and shoot him Jared."

The guy laughed, and then responded back. "Stop with the scare tactics. You're not going to shoot me."

"Yeah you're right. Kick him in the feet." As soon as the words came out of her mouth. Jared kicked the wounded man's feet. The man let out a scream in pain. Kenna looked up at Jared in surprise, and said. "I was bluffing. You should not have done that."

"Why not? I'll do it again." Jared said, as he took his foot back to kick the man again.

"Stop. Wait there are four of us. Nathan is waiting on us on the other side of the building."

"Nathan Waters?" Jared asked.

"Cuff him. We have to get Waters."

Jared looked straight at her to say. "Do I look like I have cuffs on me?"

"Fine, I'll use mine." Kenna said, and reach into her bag pulling out a zip strap. "Let me know if this is too tight." She said as she strapped the man's wrists together.

"Yes that is way too tight."

"Okay, good, let's go." She told Jared, and then the two officers started to run to the other side of the building.

"Hold it right there, and drop your guns." The two officers stopped, and looked over their shoulders to see a city cop holding a gun on them.

"Raymond. It's me. Jared."

"Jared, I'm sorry. I didn't recognize you."

"That's okay. We got to go, and get that man over by that car." After yelling out his orders they continued on. It was too late. When they rounded the corner they saw a gray Toyota Four Runner speed off.

"Damn it." Kenna said. "He got away. Again."

"I need to call Richard. He's going to love this, calling him out twice in one night." Jared told Kenna, as they were walking back over to the injured man. "Are you going to interrogate our bad guy; again."

"I'm going to talk to him." Kenna turned to face Jared, pointed her finger at him, saying. "And you stay away from him."

"What? I was able to find out about Waters, didn't I?"

"By means of torture. You want to get us in trouble?" Kenna shuck her hear, turned to walk on, then turned back to say. "Let me handle this. You just watch. Oh, and call Richard, and get him out here." Kenna walked over next to Raymond. "Has he been behaving?"

Raymond answered. "Yes, just been complaining about his restraint."

"You know. I should probably get that thing off of him. I always have trouble telling how tight I'm getting them. Has he told you anything, like who he's working with, or what their intentions are?"

Raymond shook his head before saying. "No, just said that his restraint was too tight, and that Jared had kicked his foot."

Kenna looked over at Raymond. "Oh that was an accident. Jared would never purposely kick an injured man. Now sir lets put all that behind us, and why don't you tell me why you and your colleagues tried to gun us down."

The man replied. "Like I told you before. I'm not talking."

"Fine, so you're not talking. Raymond, will you help me get him on his feet, so we can get him to your car. You just as well lock him up; he's not going to help us. Kenna said, before reaching down to take the man's arm to help him to his feet.

"Wait, I can't stand up. My ankle's broken."

"Not my problem. But getting you arrested is. Oh and by the way. Did you know that there is an innocent man lying dead in there because of you people? So don't even try to get any sympathy from me. Raymond do you mind?" Kenna looked over at Raymond.

"Oh yes. Sorry." Raymond said, and then grabbed the man's arm to help him to his feet.

"Wait, all I can tell you, is that Nathan Waters picked us up, and told us that we needed to make a hit. It was retaliation for you taking out Jeremy Black." The man finally blurted out.

"Jeremy Black is dead? Where is the body?"

"Atlanta. That is where his family is from. They're preparing him to be buried."

Kenna looked down at the man, and took a step back. "They just as well wait. That way they can bury his brother with him."

"You killed Cory too?" The man let out a little laugh. "Ohh, lady you have just opened up a big can of whoop ass. They know who you are, and they won't stop till you're dead."

Kenna leaned forward, to say. "Bring them on, and may the best woman win." Kenna started to walk away, but turned back to ask. "By the way, do you happen to know who killed Alison Conner?"

"I've never heard of her."

Kenna turned toward Jared. "Did you get a hold of Richard?"

"Yes they should be here in a little bit." Jared then asked. "How is it any different between me kicking that guy's foot, and you trying to stand him up."

"I was being helpful. You were just being mean. There's Richard now." Kenna smiled, and then pointed at the state patrol car coming down the road.

The car pulled up to Jared and Kenna with Richard stepping out of the car. "Well is this going to go on all night?"

Kenna answered him. "According to our man on the ground, it's going to go on till I'm dead."

"Well we can't let that happen. Let's see this man." Richard said, and then walked over to the man on the ground. "Drew Perry. You shoot him Kenna?"

"Yes sir, I did."

"Well you should have aimed a little higher. Who is he hired out to?" Richard addressed his question to Kenna.

"He says that Nathan Waters picked him up to kill me, for killing Jeremy Black."

"So Jeremy Black is definitely dead? And they know this, and they know that you did it?" Kenna nodded her head to Richard's question. "Yeah, well, I guess you are in some big trouble." Richard looked over at Jared to say. "Still want to hang with her?"

"Like I said before. I'm in till the end." Was Jared's answer.

"Well I didn't like the sound of that comment, Richard. You think this is all my fault. The reason that these people are coming after us?" Kenna turned away for a second, then turned back to say. "And if you think that I need to continue on my own then I will. That is fine with me."

Richard answered. "No, I think that you need to pack up, and head back to Springfield." Kenna started to comment back, but Richard interrupted, to say. "I know that you're not going to do that. Never ran from a fight before, have you?"

"No. Dad always said, that anytime that you run from a fight, your just going to always be looking over your shoulder waiting to be attacked. I started this, I'll finish it."

Richard gave Kenna a little smile. "I'll call Barry to let him know to check his body bag supply, then. You two need some rest. Why don't youns go over to the county jail, and catch some sleep. And Jared you're going to have to go see Kalley before I can let you back on the streets."

CHAPTER XII

The two officers took the advice of the superior officer, and went over to the county jail. Jared pulled up out front of the jail, and looked over to see Kenna beside him loading up a hand bag to take inside. She didn't carry very many clothes with her, so most likely her bag was filled with guns and ammunition. He took out his gun, it was empty. Reaching in the glove compartment he pulled out a second clip for the gun, and a box of forty five shells. Jared then replaced his empty clip, and started to the empty. "Are you coming, or are you just going to sit in there all night?" Jared looked over to see Kenna staring at him; he then went ahead and got out of the truck.

"Sorry I was just reloading." Jared said, as they walked in the building. Inside they met up with Leon Dow

"Could I help you two?" He asked.

"That's okay Leon." Jared said. "We're just going to crash here for a couple of hours. You want to keep a look out, for any suspicious people." When he said that, Leon got all excited, his eyes popped wide open, and he started to shake a little bit.

Kenna looked over at Jared to say. "That was cruel. You've got him all nervous."

Smiling, Jared said back to her. "Yeah, that might have been a little mean. I hope that he doesn't wet himself." Before walking to the back, Jared turned back to see Leon peeking around the edge of the window. "I kind of feel like Otis Campbell coming in here to sleep of a drunk." Jared sat down on the bed, and finished loading his clip. A brick wall separated the two cells. After loading his clip, Jared went around to talk to Kenna. She appeared to be asleep, so he went back to his bed, and lay down. He lay there in silence. It was almost too quiet. If he were at home he would have a fan running to help him go to sleep. After about five hours of sleep Jared opened his eyes, and looked around the cell. He looked at his watch; it was six o'clock in the morning. He walked over to his neighboring cell to find that it was empty, so he went on out front to find Gregg Meyers. "Hey Gregg."

"Morning Jared, how you doing this morning?"

"Okay, kinds of stiff after sleeping on that make shift bed." He looked around the room, and then asked. "Where's Kenna?"

"She left about thirty minutes ago. She didn't say anything, she just took her satchel and left." Jared stood there without responding. Gregg then asked. "You need anything?"

Jared looked over at Gregg. "No. I need to go see my therapist, so I think I'll go home and freshen up a little bit before I go." He started to walk out the door, but turned back to ask. "She didn't say where she was going or anything?"

"No, nothing at all." Gregg answered.

Jared went ahead, and headed to his house. Everything looked the same as it did the night before. There were busted windows, a couple of bullet holes in the wall, and empty casing all over the floor. Jared swept the floor, and called a carpenter friend of his. "Hey Jim are you real busy?"

"Not real busy. What do you need?" Came the voice back over the phone.

"I have a couple of busted window that needs to be replaced. How soon do you think that you can come over?"

"I'll be there in about thirty minutes." Jim answered. Jared waited around, he continued to clean up the mess, and get ready for work. "Anybody home." Came a voice from the living room. It was Jim, standing out front of the house, talking through the window. "This is nice. What did you do here?'

"Oh just a little gun fight with some bad guys." Jared walked out of the door, handed Jim a key, and said. "I have to go to work. Thanks a lot. Here's a key to the front door I can get it back from you later."

Jared went straight to Kalley's office. "Hi Terri, is Kalley busy this morning?"

"No. And Richard already called to let us know that you were coming. So just have a seat, and I will let her know that you are here." He was barely able to sit down, when Terri said. "You can go on in now."

"Jared, how are you doing?" Kalley asked.

"I'm doing well. Richard just wanted me to come in here, because I was in a couple of shoot outs yesterday. I'm feeling okay about it." Was the answer that he gave Kalley?

"Did you have to shoot anybody?"

"Yes. I thought that the first time that I would have to shoot someone, it might bother me more. It feels like it was something that I had to do to survive. Besides we were in such a rush, that I didn't have time to think about it." Jared waited for a response, before asking. "What do you think, should I feel some remorse."

Kalley thought for a minute, before saying. "Some people don't ever feel remorse. And sometimes it will hit them later, and if it does you can talk to me then. Another thing depends on the shot that you took, rather it was personal or not. Were you under fire at the time?"

Jared had to think about it, but he then answered. "Yes we were."

"When you say we what do you mean? Who was with you?"

"Kenna." He answered.

"So where was she at the time, when you shot this person?" Kalley asked.

"She was lying on the floor of the hallway, escaping the gun shots."

Kalley thought for a minute, before asking. "So you feel as though you were protecting her?"

"Yes, that is it. I guess I was protecting her."

"Do you still think that you have feelings for her?" Kalley asked.

"Yes, I think that I am at times, but then at times I think that I'm just caught up in the excitement that she has brought with her. She's young and beautiful. And look at me, I'm ten years older then she is, and not really so good looking any more."

Kalley remarked back to him. "Don't sell yourself so short. How long has it been since you have been on a date?"

"Well my wife was the last person that I dated, and that was seventeen years ago. Pretty long time, huh."

"Are you having trouble letting her go?" Kalley asked.

"I would probably say that I am having trouble letting it all go. You know of being a husband and a father. That is something that I will never be again. Besides I wasn't much of a Casanova anyways."

Kalley looked up from her tablet to say. "Really. I would not have guessed that. Being the strong football player type and all."

"That's just it. All I ever thought about was football, before I injured my knee. It's funny, but now I don't even watch football."

"Okay." Kalley said, as she looked at her watch. "I guess you need a note from me in order to get back to work." Kalley handed Jared the note. "If you have any problems, just come in or call me at any time."

"Okay. I'll do that." Jared said, as he stood up to leave. "This does help to talk to you. Thank you."

When Jared walked into the station, he went straight to Richard's office, to give him the note from his doctor. "Here you go; I'm okay to go back to work." Jared said, as he handed the note to his supervisor.

Richard looked at the note. "Yeah I guess you are. Where's your side kick?"

"I don't know. When I woke up this morning she was gone. Are there some things that you're not telling me about her? Because it feels like you know her better then what you are telling me." Jared asked his boss.

While trying to think of a good way to tell Jared. Richard folded the note, and then looked up at Jared to say. "Your right there is some things that I'm not telling you. And that's why I keep giving you the chance to get out of working with her. Which I will continue asking you. There are things that I can't tell you about her. So do you want to keep working with her?"

"Yes I do."

"Okay. I will tell you one thing. Trouble has a way of finding her. So always be on the lookout. And there she is now." Richard leaned forward, smiled, and said. "Good luck with her." Kenna walked into the room. "Morning Kenna. Anything new with you today?"

"I haven't been shot at in the last couple of hours. So what are we going to do about this drug cartel?"

Richard straightened up in his chair. "We? I'm not going to do anything about them."

Kenna's face turned red, as she leaned forward on Richard's desk to say. "So what are you going to do just turn your head like nothing happened?"

"No, I informed Claudia over at the FBI about last night." Richard leaned back forward toward Kenna. "And if you want to get involved with it, you can go join her."

Kenna turned and walked out the office door. Jared followed closely behind her. "Well are we going to go talk to the FBI?" Jared asked.

"No. There wouldn't be any point in it. They would just treat us like we were just a couple of state troupers." Kenna paused for a couple of seconds, looked back at Richard's office, and said. "We are either going to have to stay out of it, or shake things up and let it come to us. Besides we still have a murder case to solve. And all this is doing is taking our focus off of Alison."

Jared opened the door to go out of the station. As he waited for Kenna to walk through, he asked. "Don't you think that they are connected?"

"No, not at all. When I asked Nathan Waters's thug about Alison, he was completely clueless. I'm sure that if those people were involved in her death, he would at least know the name. Besides those guys were packing iron, not rope. They don't seem like the hands on type of guys." Kenna said as they were sitting down in the car. While she was sitting down, she was squirming, grunting, and making faces, while putting on her seat belt. "I hate these damn things."

Jared looked over at the young lady, while snapping his seat belt. "What the seat belt?"

"No, the vest. I feel bulky, with this damn thing on."

"Oh, I thought that something looked different about you today." Jared said, as he started the car. "Wait, should I be wearing one?"

"Yeah probably, but it wouldn't help you anyway. If somebody is going to shoot you, they are probably going to go for the head." Kenna told Jared.

"I'm probably going to get shot in the head. What about you, you're not going to get shot in the head?" Jared asked, while he put the car in reverse to back out of the parking lot.

"No, I'm pretty. They aren't going to shoot me in the face, and mess this up." Kenna explained, as she took her finger, and drew a circle around her face.

Jared stopped the car, and looked over at his passenger. "You made that up. Right?"

"No, not at all. Statistics have shown that hit men don't like to shoot pretty people, especially pretty women in the face."

Jared sat there for a few seconds, just staring at Kenna. He then put the car in park. "I think I will put one on anyways." He said, as he popped the trunk, and stepped out of the car to retrieve his vest.

"Suit yourself, but it's not going to help." After Jared was back in the car he put the car in drive. They both looked to the right, then to the left. Kenna said. "What are you waiting for, there isn't anyone coming."

"Which way? Where are we going?"

Smiling, Kenna replied. "You want to go see Barry?"

"Barry? Why Barry?"

"Because we still need to get some information on Brett's death." Kenna said, as they pulled out on the street.

"So now we're trying to solve the murder of Brett Harper."

"Brett's murder and Alison's is most likely the same person. And seeing how that Brett's murder is the freshest, then we are probably going to get more clues off of it." Kenna explained. "I guess that your shrink thinks that you're sane enough to go back to work?'

"Well, she wrote me a note. Do you think that I should feel bad about shooting that guy, last night?" Jared asked, but thought that it might be a stupid thing to do.

"Why? Was he a friend of yours?"

Jared looked over at Kenna, surprised at her question. "No, but I'm sure that he had friends, and family."

"I wouldn't worry about that. He didn't, before he came to gun us down, so I wouldn't worry it either, if I were you." The two rode along in silence, before Kenna explained to Jared. "Don't try to look into this to much, or it will eat you up. We did what we had to do to survive. And if you think that you should feel bad about killing that man, then don't. All that is going to do is slow down your reaction, and then most likely get us both killed."

CHAPTER XIII

The two officers walked into Barry's office. Barry looked up from his desk. "Well what brings you two here? Kill someone else, and dropping them off yourself?" Barry said with a little smile on his face.

Kenna replied. "What and cheat your boys out of some work. Is there any thing that you can tell us about Brett's murder?"

"Only that his murderer and Alison's were the same person. I really think that we are looking at a crime of passion here." Kenna gave Barry a look of surprise. "I don't think that Brett drugged Alison, I think that he was just passing on some drug to her."

"So you're saying that Alison was a user." Kenna said in an almost angry voice.

"That's what I'm saying. And I think that they might have been lovers too. You probably need to round up your suspects again, and question them about the relationship this time." Kenna started to walk out of the door, when Barry stopped her. "By the way, we pick up another body this morning from the hospital. You might recognize him by the holes in his ankles."

Kenna stopped, and with a surprised look on her face said. "The man that I shot in the hotel parking lot?" Barry nodded his head at her. "I didn't kill him. He was perfectly fine when I left him. All I did was shot him in the ankles."

"Slow down Missy. I don't think that you killed him either. The autopsy showed that he died of a heart attack. And maybe it was drug induced, because his heart didn't show any long term scaring. My best guess Missy is that somebody didn't want him talking." Barry stood up, and walked over to Kenna. "Missy, why don't you let this go? These are some pretty bad people. You're liable to get yourself hurt."

"I can't let it go. They're coming after me, now. And for what. All I did was shoot one of their people. Apparently somebody must have liked him pretty well. But thanks for the heads up." Kenna then turned and walked out of the office. Outside of the building she stopped, and just stood there looking around. Jared walked out of the building, and stood to her left, she then turned to face him. "A user."

"Excuse me."

"He said Alison was a user. I can't believe that." Kenna turned around, and faced the door.

"Kenna you don't know her that well. Just because she looks innocent, doesn't make her an innocent. She was probably lured in by Brett's charm. Then he probably got her hooked on drugs." Kenna turned and faced Jared, with an angry look on her face. "What. I can see that happening. Can't you?"

Kenna seemed even angrier, now. "No I can't. And the reason I can't. Son of a bitch. Get down. Here we go again." The two officers dropped down in front of the squad car just as a round of shots fired off. Most of the shots hit the back of the car, but some of them hit the glass door, shattering it. "Jared go for the door." Jared dove inside of the office. Just when he did, he heard Kenna starting to shoot. He then stood up beside the door, and pulled out his pistol. He could see that there was a man in the back, and one in the front of the passenger side of the car shooting fully automatic guns. Jared took careful aim, squeezed off two rounds, and hitting the gunman in the front seat. When he did the man in the back seat stopped shooting just long enough for Kenna to stand up,

and start firing off her Smith and Wesson forty five. After six shots she emptied her clip, within seconds reloaded, and emptied a second clip. After she fired off her last shot, the car rolled into the ditch, with the horn honking.

"Did we get them?" Jared asked.

"I think so." Kenna replied, while changing out her clip, and walking toward the gray Chevrolet Avalanche. The driver was laid over the steering wheel, with a bullet hole to the back of the head. The front seat passenger was laid across the seat, with a bullet hole to the cheek. And the man in the back seat had his throat shot out. "Yes we got them." Kenna hurried back toward the office saying. "Barry. We need to check on him."

"Barry, you okay?" Jared who was the first one into Barry's office, asked.

The old man looked up from his computer screen to say. "Yes I'm fine. How about you two?"

Kenna walked into the office. "Yeah we're both fine." Barry turned back to his computer screen. "What are you doing?" The young lady asked.

Barry peeked back from behind the computer. "I'm ordering more supplies. Things are picking up around here. And as long as you two are still here things are going to keep picking. Oh, Jimmy and Richard are on the way. I knew that you two were busy, so I went ahead, and called them."

"Thanks." Jared replied.

"Okay." Barry said as he pushed away from his desk, and stood up. "Let's go take a look at these new hoodlums." The three then walked out of the morgue. Kenna, with her hand on her pistol went out the door first, with the coroner close behind her. As they looked in the truck Barry said. "Yep they're all dead. I guess this means that I am going to have to call my brain dead helpers."

Ten minutes after the shooting was over with two county cars, and three state cars came speeding down the road. James Benson was the first to arrive, and then followed by Greg Meyers. Following them were the state police officers Richard, Clayton, and Eddy. Barry had gone back into the morgue to call the Marshal Brothers, leaving the two officers out with the dead bodies. James walked up to the car first, looked inside, without saying a word, then walked into the morgue.

"Wow what a mess." Gregg said when he looked in the truck window. "The Marshal Brothers are going to have a hay day with this one. You get one Jared?"

"Yes, the one in the face."

Gregg asked. "Lucky shot, or was that what you were aiming at?"

Jared kind of laughed, before saying. "I don't even know if I was even aiming at that guy, or not."

"Well, well, well. At least you two are saving the county some money by just shooting them in front of the morgue, so we don't have to transport them." Richard said, as he walked toward the truck.

"You're welcome." Kenna said, with a smile.

"I wasn't thanking you." Richard said.

"Then I will." Came the reply from James, as he walked back to the truck. "Recognize them. Three of the FBI's most wanted. If you ask me, the most foolish. Drive by shooting, how inaccurate is that, and with Uzis. And what the hell is that dog doing."

Everyone looked down at Sarge, who had come with Eddy, and was now digging at the passenger side door. "Eddy get that damn dog away from the truck." Richard yelled out.

"Wait a minute." Kenna said, as she started to open the door. "I bet there might be drugs in here."

Eddy grabbed Sarge, to pull him back. "I don't think that Sarge is a drug smelling dog." When Kenna opened the door Sarge's nose went right to the door panel. Kenna felt around to find a loose place in the panel. When she did, she pulled the panel off exposing bags of pills inside of the door. Eddy had a big smile on his face, as pet his dog on the head. "Good boy. I guess I have a drug sniffing dog now."

"Put the panel back on Kenna, and we did not see this. I'm calling Claudia." Richard said.

"Yeah, sure let's just hand this over to them. What are you afraid of?" Kenna asked.

Richard paused from making his phone call, to answer her. "What am I afraid of? Well first of all, getting shot, and getting everyone shot around us. I don't know if you know it or not, but we are out gunned. They are after you two, and there isn't anything I can do to help you." Richard started again to make his phone call. "And as far as those drugs go. It's going to be better if the FBI takes them, and get them off of our hands, because if the Black family decides that they want their drugs back. I don't want to be the one that has to stand in their way of getting them."

While everybody was talking over the situation, Gregg, who had been training in forensics, was going through the bodies. "What do we have here?" Everybody turned there attention towards Gregg. "It's an e-mail." He then unfolded the note, and started to read it. "Pick up Josh, and Brody, and take drugs to MT. Vernon. On the way kill the cops that killed my nephews. Also make sure that Drew isn't talking."

James said to Gregg. "Well put that back too and shut the door. I guess we know who the passengers are, and who killed Drew Perry."

"Who is Drew Perry?" Kenna asked.

"The man that you put in the hospital yesterday and is now in the morgue." James answered Kenna's question but his attention quickly turned to the cars that were coming down the road. "That was quick. What the hell, were they just down the road?"

"Yeah pretty much." Richard answered. "They had heard about the shoot out, and seeing how these two are usually involved here lately they figured out that it must have been the same bunch."

In the lead car was Claudia. She walked up next to Richard, and looked in the car. "What do you have, a couple of assassins on your team? Head shots on all three of these men."

Richard replied. "No it just worked out that way that they were shot in the heads. So when are you going to take care of this problem, so my people don't have to." Richard is able to stand up to her, and talk her down.

"May we have the crime scene, Richard?" Claudia asked.

"Yes you may, and by the way you might want to check behind the panel of the passenger door. Our drug dog already found it for you. Your welcome" Richard smugly said as he walked away.

Kenna walked along side of Richard. "Boy, you showed some balls with her." Richard stopped, and looked down at the young lady. "I mean that in a good way." The two continued to walk away from the crime scene, and toward the morgue.

"How long are the Feds going to poke around here?" Asked Berry. "I want to get them in out of this September sun as soon as possible."

Richard answered. "I have no idea. What's the matter, afraid that they're going to start stinking?" Richard walked on inside of the building, and then turned to face everybody behind him.

"I think we all need to go inside. Barry do you have any funerals today."

"No., we don't have anything going on today."

"Good let's all go into the parlor, and have a meeting." The two county officers and four state officers followed Richard to the parlor. "Now I think that everybody can agree with me that someone is passing on information on where Kenna and Jared are at all times." Nobody said a word. They were all a bit shocked, but hearing it said they now believed that it was true. Yes somewhere there is a leak, but why. "Guarantee you this. When I find who it is, they will be lying down stairs." There was silence through the crowd. Richard isn't the type of person to make a threat, but if he does you better believe that he will hold true to it.

Clayton asked. "You don't think that it is one of us inside this room, do you?"

"Why, you're not feeling guilty are you?"

"No I'm not." Clayton answered.

Richard looked around the room. "Anybody else?" Nobody spoke up. "How about you Eddy? It seems that you have been checking up on Kenna. Have you been selling her out to?"

With a look of horror on his face Eddy answered. "No. Yeah I've been checking her out. Only because I was worried about Jared. But I haven't been telling anybody where they were or anything. All I know is that she is down here on inactive duty. That was all that I questioned."

James Benson spoke up. "She is down here because Richard and I called her down here. Which now I'm thinking was a mistake."

"Yeah, well maybe. But she is already here." Said Richard. "I think you need to drop the Alison Conner case, for now."

"What." Kenna said, as she stood to her feet. "I'm not going anywhere."

"Calm down young lady." Richard informed of her. "I didn't say anything about you leaving. If that were the case I would have sent you back Wednesday, after your first shoot out. The Alison murder case doesn't have anything to do with this drug ring, does it?"

Kenna sat back down in her chair, before answering him. "No. I don't believe that it does. But why are they after Jared and me? Sure I took out one of their kinfolk, but they started it."

Richard responded to her question. "I'm not sure why they are after you. That is something that the rest of us need to find out."

Kenna said. "The rest of us?"

"No. The rest of us." Richard answered, while drawing a circle with his finger excluding Kenna.

"What am I supposed to do, just hide out while you guys are out beating the bushes?"

"Yeah I don't think that, there is any place that you can hide out at. The only other thing that you can do is what you're doing now. Make yourself visible and see what comes after you." Richard's answer might not have been the right answer, but it was the one that Kenna wanted to hear.

Jared spoke up. "This all started when we were coming out of Brett Harper's house".

"What were you doing in Brett's house?" Richard asked.

"Just snooping around." Kenna answered. "But they were already following us. Remember them checking us out at Hardees."

"That's right. We saw them first at Hardees, and again as we were coming out of Brett's."

Richard asked again. "What were you doing in Brett's house?"

"Richard. Can't you get over that?" Kenna yelled out at him. "I picked the lock; we walked in, and walked back out. That is it."

With a surprised look on his face Jared said. "You said that the lock had already been picked."

"No Jared, I picked the lock. Now we can all get over that, or somebody can arrest me." After Kenna's outburst things got very quiet. "Okay then. Sometime before we went to Hardees Jeremy Black and Nathan Waters picked up on us. So it had to have been because of us talking to somebody before that."

Barry stepped into the room. "Richard. Melvin and Mac Marshal are here. Any subjection on what I should tell them to do?"

Richard smiled. "Yeah, tell them to go stand out by the crime scene tape, and wait for the feds to get done." He then let out a little laugh. "That should hurry them up, and get their asses out of here quicker."

"Okay I'll tell them." Barry walked away smiling.

"The only people that we talked to besides Barry, and Jimmy out side of the state police, were Jordan Lane, and Mike, and Sharon Davis." Kenna explained.

Jared said. "Yeah. If Mike has any connection with this drug ring, he might have called the hit on you. You did kick his ass, and pull a gun on his wife."

"Oh shit, I don't even want to know it." Richard said as he lowered his head. "Is there anybody else, that either one of you two have talked to?"

Jared answered. "My therapist."

Gregg asked. "You're seeing a shrink. Are you okay?"

"Yes, it's policy."

"Policy for what?" Gregg asked.

"Because of the shootouts that I have been involved with." Jared answered.

Eddy spoke up. "You were seeing her before the shootouts. He was having nightmares, because of finding Alison's dead body."

"I sent him to see the therapist. And that has nothing to do with this case. So please can we stay on track." Richard yelled out. "Eddy, you and Clayton take your drug sniffing dog to the movie place, and ask around. Now Clayton, you need to watch the reactions of the employees, when you announce that you have a drug sniffing dog. If there are drugs being sold out of there, they are going to want to see a warrant. If they do, Eddy you need to get Sarge excited. Stick a hot dog in your pocket; I don't know what ever it takes. Then tell them that you will be back with a warrant."

Clayton smiled and nodded his head. "Okay got that can do."

"Copy that." Eddy responded.

"Gregg, why don't you have your cousin hack into the video feed to the store, so we can watch the scramble?" Richard informed the county officer.

Gregg turned red, started to sweat, and stutter. "Ah, ah, I'm not sure what you are talking about."

"Oh come on we all know that he can do it. He's the best in the area. Nobody can catch him. All he has to do is set us up with a feed somewhere. Hell we don't even have to see him. What do you say, can you do it?" Richard asked the officer.

"Okay he's not going to get in any trouble is he?"

"Like I said, I don't even have to see him. And I won't have idea of where the feed is coming from." Gregg walked out of the door, without saying a thing. "Good. Now for you two, I think that you need to go see the Davis again."

With a smile on her face, Kenna agreed to it. "So what are you two going to do?"

Richard answered. "We will be watching to see what unfolds. Most likely somebody is going to get rattled."

"Hey Kenna." She turned to look at James, who had called out her name. "Why don't you and Jared stay at my house tonight?"

"Okay, thank you."

James then said. "Be careful sweetheart." Kenna smiled at James before walking out the door.

Once they were outside, they saw the Marshal Brothers standing beside the crime scene tape asking questions. "So how do we become FBI agents? We're really good with dead bodies." Mac lifted the tape up over his head. "Let me come in and show you." This was the closest that either one of them had been the whole time. "Holy shit Melvin, look at these kill shots." Melvin started to move closer to the car.

"If you two don't get back behind that line, and stay there. There is going to be two more dead bodies out here." Claudia yelled out at the two brothers, and then turned back to her team. "Are we about done here?"

One of the officers answered. "I think so, let's let the morons get the bodies out, and then we can take the truck back to our lab."

"Did he call us morons Melvin?" Mac asked.

"I think he did. I don't think we want to be FBI, they're assholes. Come on lets get them out of here." The two brothers opened the door to the passenger's side. Melvin grabbed a set of legs, and started to pull, at that point Mac grabbed arms, and the two started to carry the man into the building.

"Stop you idiots." It was Barry, who was now standing in the doorway." Look at that, his head is dragging the ground, and leaving a blood trail. You're not bringing him in here like that. I gave you three body bags what did you do with them."

"Oh yeah, I'll get them." Mac said, as he dropped the body, and headed back to the SUV to get the body bags, that were provided to them. "I don't know why we're wasting these bags."

"It doesn't matter what you think. Just do what you are told." Barry yelled out at the two brothers. "When you two get done moving those bodies you're going to clean up all of this blood." Barry then turned, and walked back into the building.

"I think we really pissed him off this time Mac."

CHAPTER XIV

Kenna and Jared pulled up in front of Mike Davis's house, just as Mike was getting out of his car. Mike walked over to the passenger side of the state police car. "What do you want now?"

"We would like to know why we are being targeted by Nathan Waters." Kenna replied.

Mike looked around, and then leaned down to say to Kenna. "Meet me at the Holliday Inn. I don't want to talk here."

The two officers drove about two miles down the road to the Holiday Inn, with Mike Davis close behind them. Once they were at the hotel Mike drove to the back, to make sure that they weren't able to be seen very well. Mike parked his car, and went over to the state patrol car. "Okay, what is this all about?" Kenna asked.

"Just drive Jared." Jared drove toward the highway, and then stopped before pulling out. "Turn, and go out toward the country. You two trying to get me killed too?"

Kenna quickly turned around, with an angrier look on her face. "I'm not even trying to get myself killed. So what do you know about all of this?"

"I know that you should not have killed Jeremy Black, because now you have pissed them off."

With anger still in her voice she asked. "They were shooting at us. What was I supposed to do?"

"You could have just ducked for cover." Mike explained.

"I guess I don't know how you people work down here. You just let the bad guys shoot at you, you let them go, and then it's all good. Huh." Kenna said, before turning back around to face the front of the car.

"Yeah that's pretty much how it works."

Now even more mad, Kenna turned back around, to voice her opinion. "Ya'll are just a bunch of dumb ass hicks down here then. That is not the way that I operate."

"You missed one thing. We're a bunch of live dumb ass hicks. Besides, what the hell do you think that we're supposed to do? We're out gunned and out manned down here. I already lost my first wife trying to get rid of this shit, once. I think I've paid my dues." Mike then sat back, and looked out of the driver's side window.

"It might have been easier for you to have gotten out of this, and then it will be for me. Apparently the only way I'm getting out is in a body bag, being drug around by the Marshal Brothers. The only chose I have is to stand my ground, and fight back."

"Why don't you just leave, and let the feds take care of it?" Mike asked.

"Because I don't run, that's why. And where am I supposed to go. They have eyes on me every where. Who knows, you might be a pair of those eyes." Kenna looked back at him to see him get riled up.

Instead, Mike just smiled, and said. "No, not hardly. I've learned to keep my distance from those people."

Not getting the response that she thought that she might, Kenna toned down a bit. "I just thought that it was awful peculiar that Nathan

Waters, and Jeremy Black would start following us, shortly after we left your house."

"No. They checked you out at Hardees. Then when you came out of Brett's house that was what pissed them off." Mike explained.

"And how do you know all of this?"

"I hear things. And besides, what were you doing in Brett's house?" Mike asked, with a smug voice.

Knowing that she had been caught again, and looking like the cat that ate the canary. Kenna tried to explain. "We were just snooping around. We were on a murder investigation." "Yeah, well. How's that going?"

"Not very well. I'm a bit distracted from the case right now. And you said that they were checking us out at Hardees?" Kenna asked she then faced the front of the car again.

"That's singular. Just you." Mike sat back, and looked out the window again.

Turning back around, with a surprised look on her face Kenna asked. "Me? What were they checking me out for?"

"I don't know. I guess they were a little jumpy that there's a new cop in the area." Mike laughed a little, and then said. "I guess they had a good reason to be jumpy, too." Still facing the back of the car, Kenna noticed that a car was starting to pass them. That's dumb, what kind of an idiot passes a police car. "I wish that there were more that I could tell you, but."

Kenna cut him off by yelling out. "Gun." Jared quickly looked to his left, saw a man pointing a gun out of the window of a Chevy Tahoe; he then slammed on the breaks. As he did the car went ahead of them. The gunman shot, but none of the shots came close to them. "He's getting ready to shoot again." Kenna yelled out. Jared slammed on the gas, rammed the back of the SUV, causing the gunman to loose his gun. But seeing how that the SUV was a little taller then the police car. The front end of the car went under the Tahoe, catching the Tahoe's bumper on the car's grill guard.

"Now I've got them." Jared said, before slamming on the breaks. White smoke came from all four of the car tires, as they came to a stop. The driver of the SUV put the car in reverse, in order to back up onto squad car. At the same time the passenger opened the door, and was pointing a gun at the officers.

"He's going to try to shoot again." As soon as the words came out of her mouth Jared put the car in reverse. This jarred the Tahoe, causing the gunman to fall out of the car, and in turn unhooking the two vehicles. Once that they were unhooked the passenger from the SUV was trying to get into the Tahoe. At that point Jared put the car in drive, mashed the gas, and rammed into the back of the SUV again.

"Oh shit here we go again." Came a voice from the back seat. This time when he hit the Tahoe the grill guard matched up with the bumper, pushing the car down the road. The passenger was unable to get back into the SUV. As they went by him Kenna opened the door knocking him to the ground. At the same time she bailed out of the car close to the bad guy. The dazed man started to get to his feet, but Kenna was quicker getting to her feet. She jumped up, and dropped kicked her counterpart, with both feet to the chest. The man went to the ground gasping for air. Kenna quickly rolled him over, put his hands behind his back, and zip tied them.

"Get up, we're walking." She said, as she helped the man to his feet. Jared had pushed the SUV off into the ditch. He then went up to the door, pulled his gun, and was holding the driver at gun point.

"Get out of the car, while I'm still in a good of enough mood that I don't shoot you." The man unlatched the door, and Jared stepped back one step. "That's it nice and easy." Jared told the man, and then looked down the road at his partner, who was walking up the road. When he took his eyes off of his prisoner, the man came up with a gun. Jared has a wide peripheral vision, so he saw the gun coming out. He then took the butt of his own gun, and hit the man square in the middle of his forehead knocking him out cold. Jared looked down at the man saying,

"Now what the hell was that about?" He then looked back at Kenna, who was almost up to them. "You okay."

"Yeah I'm good, but you're going to have a bitching of a time getting him out from underneath that car." Kenna told Jared, he then looked down at the man, who did yes pass out, and slide under the car.

"Are you two going to let me out of this car?" Mike asked. Kenna walked over to let the big man out of the back seat of the car. "Thank you."

"I wouldn't be so quick to thank me. Jared needs some help, getting his guy out from under that car." Mike was giving her a funny look, as he was getting out of the car. "What? I'm sure that you don't think that I'm going to help him, do you? I already got my man."

"Man he is out cold. And you hit him with the butt of your gun?" Mike asked, as he reach down to help Jared pull on the man.

"Yeah, I heard about a guy doing that once, and I always wanted to try it. Works great doesn't it." Jared explained, as they pulled the man up to the road. Jared looked over at Kenna, who was just hanging up her phone. "You call Richard?"

"Yes, I did. He said that Clayton, and Eddy were done, and that he could send them over to us." Kenna, who was sitting on the hood of the car said.

"Well now that we have this guy up out of the ditch, and you have help on the way. I think that I will just walk back to Hucks, and have someone pick me up there." Mike explained, before starting to walk back up the road.

With a surprised look on his face Jared said. "Wait Mike you don't have to leave."

"Yeah, yeah I believe that I need to leave. Quite honestly I believe that I would just like to get away from you two. Hanging around you two isn't healthy." Mike started to walk off, but turned back to say. "And hey, if you ever feel the need to talk again, please just call." Mike gave them a thumbs up. "Okay."

"That was rude." Kenna said, as she watched Mike walk off up the road. She looked down at her captured man, and asked. "I wouldn't suppose you would want to tell me who sent you, would you?"

"Go to hell lady."

"Well that's a definite no. It doesn't matter anyways. I already know who sent you, and he is probably going to send someone to kill you off anyway. So talk or don't talk you're screwed either way you want to go." Kenna sat back, and watched Jared search his man over, and cuff him. She then looked back up the road to see two state police cars, with their lights on, coming down the road. "Here comes the cavalry."

"That was quick. They must have not been to far away." Jared said, as he watched them pull up.

Clayton pulled up beside Jared. "Why is there a city officer walking up the road, back there?"

"That's Mike Davis. He doesn't want to hang with us any longer." Jared explained.

"Well Richard wants you two to take these two to the county jail. We'll stay here, and clean up the mess." Clayton explained.

Kenna patted the car that she was sitting on. "Well this is part of the mess. It's bleeding."

Jared bent over, and looked under the car, just at the time that Eddy was walking up. "So uh, do you think that I could borrow one of you two's cars?"

Clayton said. "You're not taking my car."

Jared looked over at Eddy, who said. "Yeah, you can take my car. Sarge and I can ride back with Clayton."

"That dog isn't getting in my car."

Jared smiled, looked over at Kenna, and then lend over to pet Sarge. "He can ride with us. Can't he Kenna."

"Yeah sure, there will be room for him in the back seat with these two." Kenna stood to her feet, grabbed her bad guy, and helped him to his feet. "Come on we're leaving now. By the way is there a name that I can call you."

100

"You can call me what ever you want, but I'm not giving you my name." The guy said.

"Okay then I'll just call you dumbass then." Kenna said, as she was helping him into the car.

"Come on Sarge. You can ride in the middle." Jared said, as he was half way dragging his partially conscious man. "And I will let you have a window seat." Jared turned back toward His fellow officers. "I think that there are a couple of guns along side of the road. You might want to pick them up." He said, before sitting down inside of the car.

Now Sarge doesn't usually have to share the back seat with anyone, so he wasn't too happy with the intruders that were in his space. He tried to sat up in the middle of the car, but that didn't work. He lie down across the seat with his head in one mans lap, but even that wasn't comfortable. He stood up, with his butt in one man's face, and facing the other man. He started to growl.

"Is this damn dog going to bite me?" The man asked.

Jared answered him. "I don't think so. I don't think that he has ever bitten anybody. Of course there is always the first time. What was your name again?"

"You can kiss my ass. I'm not telling you, my name either." The man said. This must have irritated Sarge, because he then let out a loud bark.

"Easy Sarge." Jared calmly said. "What do you call him, Kenna?"

"I call him dumbass. Or you can call him dead man, because when Nathan Waters finds out that he ratted on him. He's going to kill him." Kenna smiled at Jared.

"What are you talking about lady? I'm not going to rat him out. I'm not that stupid. He has eyes and ears everywhere."

The other man spoke up. "She's right Clint. We're probably dead anyways. Look what happened to Drew. They killed him to keep him from talking."

Clint yelled out at the other man. "Good going John!!! You just give them my name." Disturbed by the yelling Sarge barked again.

John yelled back. "Yeah. That's right my name is John Hickson, and this is my brother Clint." Disturbed again by the yelling Sarge turned, faced John, and started to bark again.

"Ouch. This damn dog stepped on my balls." Clint yelled out

"Now see what a little friendly conversion and a German Shepard can get you." Jared said to Kenna.

Kenna replied. "Yes I do, and I'm getting every bit of it." She held a recorder up off of the seat.

The bickering and barking continued all the way to the county jail. Once that they arrived Jared, and Kenna stepped out of the car, walked toward the jail leaving the two men in the car, with the dog.

"Hey." Clint yelled out. "You're not going to leave us in here with this dog. Are you?"

Jared walked back to the car, and opened the door. "Oh my apologies. Come on Sarge." After letting the dog out of the car he started to shut the door.

"Wait a minute. What about us?" Clint asked.

"As soon as you two calm down. We'll bring you in. But right now it's not safe for you. You two have gotten on Kenna's nerves, very badly." It was all that Jared could do to keep from laughing, while he shut the door. Kenna had left the recorder running in the front seat, in hopes of getting some more information.

When Jared walked into the station, Kenna was talking to James, and Richard. "They are a couple more of Waters hit men. Where are they all coming from? Never in my life have I ever even heard of there being this many hits being put on any cops."

Jim spoke up. "Yeah, this defiantly isn't good at all. Did you happen to get their names?"

"Yes Clint and John Hickson. Sarge got it out of them. And I left a recorder running in the front seat of the car, just incase they would want to give up some more information." Kenna explained. When Sarge heard his name, he walked over to Kenna. She lends down to pet him. "You're such a good police dog. Aren't you boy?"

"I'm going to have to hand them over to Claudia." Richard said, as he picked up the phone to call the FBI. "Clayton and Eddy are going to go over their car before we hand it over. Good afternoon Claudia. I don't suppose that you heard that we have a couple of more bad guys, have you?"

Claudia who was on the other end of the phone call, answered him. "I might have heard some rumor of your officers getting in another gun fight."

"Don't bull shit me. I'm sure that you already have agents on the scene right now. And I bet you would like to have the two men that we arrested."

"Yeah, you know we are. We've already sent your two men home, and taken over the scene. Now, what did you do with the two men that you arrested?" Claudia asked.

Richard answered. "You can pick them up at the county jail." He hung up the phone, and then turned to Kenna. "We need to go ahead and bring them in, and make sure that you pocket the recorder before the Feds get here."

Kenna went out to the car with Jared, and Gregg. The two men took the bad guys in, while Kenna retrieved her recorder. Coming down the road were Clayton and Eddy followed by another car. It was the Feds. Either they made a quick trip, after talking to Richard, or they were already following Clayton and Eddy the whole time. Kenna walked on into the station, and while walking past Richard she said. "Claudia's boys are here."

Richard looked back at her in surprise. "Already. I just talked to her."

"They followed Clayton, and Eddy."

"Alright then." Richard said, as he looked over the room. "Escort these two back out, and hand them over. The sooner we get rid of the Feds the better."

"Come on, let's go back out." Jared told the two men. As he started to walk back out of the door, he met Clayton, and Eddy. "Did you bring some guest with you?"

Eddy asked. "What are you talking about?"

"The Feds that followed you." Clayton walked on into the building to talk to Richard, while Eddy had stayed back talking to Jared. Eddy walked back out of the building to see who Jared was talking about. At the same time Jared was ushering the two men out of the door.

"Those are Feds." Eddy said, as he turned back to face Jared. Kenna knew that they had screwed up. She jumped to her feet to run out of the door. It was too late. Two men stepped out of the car, and started to spray gun fire.

"Get back inside." Jared yelled out. It was too late for Eddy. He had taken a bullet to the back, and the two prisoners had been shot as well. Jared took one to the chest as well, knocking him back in the door.

"Get him back." Kenna yelled out, before stepping out of the door way, and firing of shots at the two men. She might have hit one, or might not have, but they dove back in the car, and sped off. Kenna emptied her clip, reloaded, and then emptied it again taking out every window in the car. She looked over at Eddy lying on the ground, in a pool of blood. She started to shake. "Get an ambulance here, Eddy has been shot."

Richard ran out of the door, to the aid his officer. "Eddy can you hear me, hold on, help is on the way. Eddy. Eddy. Damn it. I hope you killed those bastards Kenna."

"No. No. Don't say that. He's not gone, is he?" Kenna already knew the answer to her question, before she asked it. She started to shake even worse now. "It's all my fault. He shouldn't be dead."

"No. It's not your fault. They're the ones that brought this, and we're going to finish it." Richard took out his phone. "Claudia, where are your people at?"

"They should be there at anytime. Why, you sound upset?" She asked.

"We were under an attack again, and I have a man down. You need to be on the lookout for a car that has been shot up. And we lost our witnesses." Richard explained to the agent.

Kenna looked over at Richard. "Jared. Is he okay?" She didn't wait for an answer. Instead she ran into the building to check on him. Inside of the building, she found Jared lying on the floor holding his chest. "You okay?"

"Yeah the vest stopped the bullet." Jared sat up, with a little smile to face said. "I guess it was a good thing that I was wearing it." Kenna smiled back at him, but her smile quickly faded, when he asked. "Eddy okay?"

"No. He took two to the back. I'm sorry, he didn't make it."

"Can you help me up? I need to see my friend. "Jared asked. Once that he was to his feet, he walked outside. Jared walked past the Hickson brothers, who were lying dead on the ground. In front of him he could see his old friend lying on the ground. Richard and Clayton stood over him, and Sarge had laid down beside him. "I can't believe that we let our guard down. You big dumb blond. You saw that they weren't Feds, so why did you turn your back on them."

"Here comes the ambulance." Kenna said, as she saw lights coming down the road. Behind it was Barry, and the Marshal Brothers.

Barry walked up to the big man lying on the ground. "This is a tragedy. How could anything like this happen. What are we going to do about this, Richard?"

"Oh we'll get them." Was his answer.

"Get who. You don't even know who they are, or how many there are of them." Pointing his finger at Richard, and in a angry voice, he said. "We've suffered a great loss here, and I don't want to see this again." He bent down to look at the officer. "Melvin, help me turn him over."

"Yes sir." Melvin said, as he gently turned Eddy over. Sarge didn't budge, he stayed at his friend's side. The bullets didn't exit the body. Most likely they were hollow points, that only had one purpose, and that was to kill.

Putting his fingers on Eddy's neck. Barry said. "I think we can get him out of here now." He called to the paramedics. "Bring your stretcher over here. I want for you to transport the body. I don't want him in the meat wagon with these two."

The paramedics, and the Marshel brothers carefully placed him on the stretcher, and put him in the ambulance. After he was loaded Mac, and Melvin came back to assist Barry. Sarge was lying beside Eddy's pool of Blood. The three year old dog was lost without his owner.

"Gregg, would you mind taking these two to the state office." Richard asked of the county officer. "We need to get them somewhere safer. What do you think James?"

"Yeah, but I don't think that the state office is going to be any safer then this place." James replied.

"So what are you saying, keep them here."

"No. I think that they need to go to my place. Gregg go ahead and take them to the state office, so they can get some transportation. Seeing how you are starting to run low on squad cars." Both Eddy's, and Clayton's cars had been shot up during the shoot out.

Richard looked over at the two cars. "Yeah, I believe we are running out of cars. But your place. Do you think that is going to be safe for you?"

"Let them try to get these two down there. Besides, I was the one that brought Kenna in on this mess. It's the least that I can do is provide her with a place to stay." Upon James' request Gregg, Kenna, and Jared loaded up in Gregg's car to go to the state office. As they were leaving two FBI cars pulled into the parking lot.

"It's about time that you showed up." Richard said.

Claudia was getting out of her car. "We've been a little busy with your shooters.

"You found them?"

"Yes, they didn't get very far. The passenger was dead, and the driver was still alive, but he was unconscious. I doubt that he makes it." Claudia explained.

"You say that like it is a bad thing." Richard said.

"It is if we are going to stop all of this. We're going to need witnesses, you know. Do you have any identification on these two?"

"Well sort of." Richard said. "They said that they were Clint, and John Hickson. Does that tell you anything."

"No, not at all. We'll have to run the names. Now Richard, why don't you let us work a little closer with youns." Claudia said with a smile on her face. She knew that they weren't telling them everything.

"I don't know what you're talking about. I think that we have kept you pretty well informed." Richard was starting to squirm.

"Yeah well, so where is Jared, and Kenna at?"

Richard answered with another question. "Why do you ask?"

"Why, because it looks as if you are trying to keep them away from us, and maybe I would like to talk to them."

CHAPTER XV

As they were going to the state office, Kenna took out the recorder that she had left recording in the car, with the Hickson Brothers. Kenna rode along in the back seat with Sarge, who just lie there in mourning. "What do you say that we listen to this, and see what those two had to say." Sarge sighed. "I'll take that as a yes." Kenna said as she pressed the play button.

The first voice that they heard was Clints. "What are they going to do just leave us out here all night?"

"I told you that we should not have taken this job." John said.

Clint replied. "I didn't take the job. I didn't have any chose, Ronald called me up, and said come up here and get rid of her. He said that she was messing everything up, and that she knows too much."

All eyes turned on Kenna. "What are you two looking at?" She asked the two men, then looked over at Sarge, who was also staring at her.

"What were they talking about, that you knew too much?" Jared asked.

Kenna was just as surprised as the guys were, at the remark. "I don't have any idea what he's talking about. Let me play some more of this." She said, as she pressed the play button.

"They should have took care of her when she was in Atlanta." John Said. "I knew she was trouble when Ronald was messing around with her."

Kenna paused the recording. "They aren't even talking about me. And who is this Ronald that they keep talking about?"

"I don't know. I'll have to get with Richard, and see if he can find out anything." Jared said. "So if you're not the one that they are after, then who are they really after, and how did they confuse you, with whoever this person is."

"That's the stupidest thing that I've heard. I suppose you think that there is another black woman that looks just like me, that they've mistaken as me. And who is this woman suppose to be?" Kenna said, before starting the recorder again.

Jared asked, before she was able to push the play button again. "Think about it they were following us, before you were even able to draw suspicion to yourself."

"I drew suspicion. And just where are you getting that from?"

Jared turned, and looked at Kenna, to say. "You did break into Brett's house." Jared turned back to face the front of the car, hoping that she didn't retaliate.

"Are you people ever going to let that go." Kenna pushed the play button.

"I tried to tell him that she was DEA, or FBI, but he didn't want to believe it."

"I think we need to get this back to Richard. Maybe he can find out who the mystery woman is." Kenna said, before turning the recorder back on.

The next thing they heard was Clint saying. "Here they come back after us."

"That is all that we have." Kenna said. "Pretty slim. I was hoping that we would get more out of them."

Once they arrived at the state police station, Kenna went straight to her car, and Sarge followed her. Jared went to his truck, then turned back to talk to Kenna. "Do you need to follow me to James' house?"

"No, he has given me directions. You can just meet us there, if you need to go somewhere first."

"Yeah, I would like to run by my house first." Jared said and then just kind of stood there. "What? Do you want me to go with you?"

Jared thought for a moment. In a way he really didn't want to be separated from her, but he didn't want to sound wimpy, and admit to it. "No. I'll be okay on my own. I just wanted to run by my house to get a few things, and see if the carpenter has finished yet."

"Okay, I'll go with you. You have beer there, and I sure could use one right now." Kenna said, as she was getting in her car.

When they arrived at Jared's house the windows had been replaced, and Jim had left. Kenna stepped out of her car, then let Sarge out of the back seat. Jared led the way to the front door. "Looks like everything is all put back together." He said, as he opened the door for them to go in. He took a bowl out of the cabinet, filled it with water for Sarge, and then grabbed two beers from the refrigerator.

"You know, I can't stop thinking about our talk with Mike Davis. Katy said that he was the city cop that talked to her. And he didn't ever mention it either times that we talked to him. And you know something, both times that we met with him we were shot at."

Jared popped the top off of the beers, handed one to Kenna. "So are you suspecting him of something?"

"I'm not too sure of what I am suspecting. But what do you think? And besides, he sure knew a lot about us. (I hear things.) That was his answer, now what's that suppose to mean." Kenna asked before taking a drink from her beer. Jared had an Illinois sock cap lying on the counter, Kenna picked it up and put it on her head saying. "I'm going to keep this."

Jared smiled then took a drink of his beer. "I know that it all sounds suspicious. I'm almost thinking that we need to talk to Mike again. I have his phone number do you want to call him?"

"No, not right now. Besides that, I'm ready to get out of here. I would hate to see your place get shot up again." Kenna tipped her beer up, and downed it. "You ready." She watched Jared as he tried to finish of his beer. He knew that he was being watched, and was trying not to wimp out.

Upon slamming the empty down on the counter he said, with watery eyes. "Okay let's go."

"Sorry about that. That must have hurt."

"I'll be fine. I don't chug beers very often any more." Jared said, as they left the house. Jared took the lead as the two drove on to James Benson's home out in the country. When they pulled up in the drive way they were met by a couple of dogs. One was an Australian Shepard, and the other was a little mutt. Jared tried to distract the dogs, while Kenna took Sarge out of the car, and into the house.

At the door waiting on them was Mae Benson. "Those damn dogs aren't bothering you, are they?" Kenna just smiled at her as she walked past.

"No they're fine." Jared said. "Mae this is Kenna Jenkins from out of the Springfield area."

With a funny look on her face, Mae held out her hand to greet Kenna. "Hi it's nice to meet you. Jimmy said that you would be coming. Jared I'm sorry to hear about Eddy. Weren't you two pretty close?" She asked, and at that time they could hear a car pull up out side.

"Yes, he has always been a good friend of mine, since he joined the force five years ago." Jared said, then turned around to see the front door open up.

A stocky gentleman in his upper twenties walked through the door. When he saw Kenna a big smile went across his face. "Chocolate Drop. What is my favorite cousin doing down here?"

There was a look of surprise across everyone's face when the big man went over to wrap his arms around Kenna. Kenna said to Jared. "I need to explain something. Jarren that is enough, put me down." She said to the big man. "Jared I would like for you to meet Jarren."

While shaking hands, Jared said. "Jarren Benson. It's nice to meet you."

"So, I guess you know who he is?" Kenna asked.

"Yeah, sure, I know who Jarren Benson is. Just the second best running back in the area." Jared said.

"What?" Jarren said. "Second best and I suppose you think that you were the best?"

"Yes I do, and it is good to meet you." Jared then turned to face Kenna. "So that would make James and Mae."

Kenna interrupted. "My aunt and uncle."

Mae then wrapped her arms around Kenna saying. "Now let me give you a proper greeting. Jimmy's been telling me about what has been going on, with all of the shootings. Sweetheart, I've been worried to death about you."

"I'm okay. Us Jenkins women are pretty tough, you know."

Jarren asked. "So have you found the son of a bitch that killed Alison?"

"No." Kenna answered his question, but then turned to Jared to say. "There's one other thing that I need to tell you. Alison was our cousin."

"Well now that would have been nice to have known." Jared said.

"Jared I didn't know you well enough to tell you."

Jared lashed out. "You mean that you didn't trust me enough."

Kenna got back into his face. "No I didn't. I know this area down here, and I know how you people are. You can't do a damn thing without pissing off the locals, and people just turn their heads, and let shit go on. Besides you know as well as I do, that if anybody found out that I was related, then I would be pulled off of the case. Then it would be just swept away, to be forgotten about." She took a step closer to Jared. "And I was not going to let that happen."

There was about a two minute hush, before Jared said. "So that's why you are on personal leave of absence." Kenna didn't answer. Instead she just nodded. Jared turned to face Jarren to give him more of an answer to his question. "We've been told to put the case on hold, until we get this drug gang off of our asses."

"Oh." Jarren said, then asked Kenna. "Is that the locals that you were talking about?"

"Yeah, they have been a nuisance. We can't seem to get anything done, without them chasing us down, and shooting at us." Kenna explained.

Jared face lit up. "Hey. By the way, you said that this vest wouldn't help. Well guess what it did. Ha. She said that I was most likely to get shot in the face, but she wouldn't."

Mae cut in. "Of course not. She's too pretty. No body is going to want to shoot her in the face."

Kenna smiled at Jared. "You want to know who made me the way that I am." She put her arm around the short woman. "You're looking at her."

"I would have thought that Jeffery and I might have had something to do with the way that you turned out." Jarren said. "We did pretty much take care of you when you were down here."

"Take care of me. You two were mean to me."

"Maybe a little bit, but we made you strong." Jarren said. "And look at the skills that we taught you."

"What, by trying to feed me to the coyotes?"

"You had a gun."

Jared was trying to figure out what they were talking about, so Kenna turned to him to say. "One night, when our parents were out, they took me out to a deer gut pile. They then through a deer hide over me and left me out there with a twenty two pistol. I couldn't come back until I killed a coyote."

Jarren cut in. "Yeah, then our parents came home early. Purdy was pissed. I can still remember her getting right up in our faces, and saying. 'You get out there and get my little girl.' I don't think Jeffery was as scared as I was."

"Oh please." Kenna said. "Jeffery's never been scared of anything. And how did you find me?"

Jarren stood there for a few seconds, as to be thinking. "Let me see. How did we find you?" Kenna gave him a look as if she was going to beat the crap out of him. "Oh yeah, I remember. I was just joking. The four of us were walking down the fence row, to find her, when we met her coming up the fence row dragging a coyote. Jeffery was very proud of you." Everybody was quiet.

"So where is Jeffery?' Jared asked.

"We don't know." Mae said, with a little tear in her eye. "He's in Special Forces, and we think that he might be in Afghanistan. We've not heard from him in almost a year."

"If I know him." Kenna said, while putting her arm around her aunt. "He's probably standing over a Taliban gut pile waiting for them to come after him."

A voice came from out of the kitchen. "I wouldn't doubt that one bit. He's just that mean." Everyone turned to see James, who had snuck in threw the back door. "You people need to more on alert."

"I knew you were back there, Jimmy." Mae said, while James went over to give his wife a kiss.

"I'm guessing that since your telling family stories, that you've filled Jared in on the family."

James asked. After seeing a couple of heads nod, James turned to Jared. "I'm sorry that we didn't tell you earlier, but we had to keep this on the down load. I made a promise to my sister-in-law and brother-in-law, that I would find out who killed my little niece. And I had to bring Kenna down here to help out. I knew that she would shake things up, but not quite this bad."

Kenna asked James. "Did we miss anything back at the county jail?"

"Well, for one thing. The feds found our shooters about a mile down the road from the station. The passenger was dead, and the driver died in a shoot out with the feds. Kind of odd, huh?" "How do you mean?" Kenna ask.

"Not that the passenger was dead. But that the other guy would get in a shoot out with the feds. Either he wanted to die, or maybe he didn't even shoot back. I'm getting a bit leery of this whole mess, with Claudia Beckham and all. They swoop in and take everything, like they don't want us to know anything." James turned his attention to Jarren. "What are you doing down here?"

"I came down to see my little cousin. They will be okay up there in Cook County with out me for a couple of days." Jarren answered his dad's question. He then turned to Jared to explain. "I work for the District Attorney's office up there. I put bad guys away too."

"We left Clayton and Eddy with enough time to search the Hickson's brothers' car. Did they find anything?" Jared asked.

James answered. "No. They didn't really have enough time to do any searching. Claudia and her gang were on them bout as soon as you left. Don't ask me how. We didn't ever call them."

Kenna said. "Kind of points back to Davis, doesn't it Jared?"

"Yes it does. He's the only other person that knew about our little incident." Jared said. "Are you getting anything off of the cameras at the video store?"

"Oh yeah. They've been on the phone, and people have been in and out of there pretty heavy. You mentioned Mike Davis. Well Mrs. Davis has came up missing. They seem pretty pissed that she didn't show up for work." James said.

"Listen to this." Kenna said, as she took the recorder out of her bag. She then played back the conversation that the Hickson brothers had, without knowing that they were being taped.

"That was interesting." James said, once the recording was done playing. "So who is this mystery woman, and who is Ronald?"

Jared said. "I was thinking that we might get this back to Richard. He probably would be able to find out for us."

"Yes, I agree." James said. "Mae what's for supper, I'm bout to starve?"

"I've been thawing some catfish, so I guess I better get started on it. I don't want my big man to starve to death." Mae said, as she kissed her husband on the mouth in passing.

CHAPTER XVI

The next day they all met at the county office again. Richard had sent Clayton to bring in Mike Davis, so they could talk to him, and at the same time he had Claudia come in. Kenna rode in with Jared, they were the last to arrive.

"Okay, we're all here now." Richard said. "Do you have the recorder with you, Kenna?"

Kenna answered him. "Yes I do." Kenna handed it over to Richard. Richard pushed the play button, and everyone gathered around to listen. "That's all of it." Kenna said, once the recording was over with.

"Well that's interesting." Richard said. "Mike, Claudia, do either one of you have anything to add to this."

Mike and Claudia looked at each other, before Claudia said. "No I, ah I don't think so." She then turned back to face Mike, who was keeping silent.

"Oh come on you two, don't jerk me around. Claudia, you have been wanting me to keep you in the loop of what was going on with us, so I think you need to keep me in the loop." After Richard said that, still nobody was talking. "Mike, who is Ronald?"

Mike didn't even try to get out of the question. "Ronald, that's one of the head guys from out of Atlanta."

"From out of?" Richard asked. "You mean that he is not still down there now?"

"No, last I knew. He was in the St. Louis area. That is who Nathan Waters answers to."

Richard asked. "So who is the woman that they are talking about. Apparently it's not Kenna."

Mike looked over at Claudia. "You want to answer that one?"

"That's classified. I can't tell you anything about her." Claudia answered.

"So, you're not going to cooperate with us."

Claudia looked back at Richard, with a surprised look on her face. "No you don't understand. I know that the FBI has, or had somebody undercover in there. But I don't know who she is, or anything about her. There was somebody feeding us information, but it all stopped. Either she was pulled out, or just went silent, or even dead. And no, they don't thing Kenna is her, they know who she is."

"What is that suppose to mean?" Richard asked.

"Oh just as soon as she came down here poking around, they put a tail on her." Claudia said. "I mean I don't have a problem with her being down here. She is stirring things up pretty good. It's like she is bringing the roaches out of the wood work." Claudia looked over at Kenna, and smiled.

"Well, I don't like for my people being bait, and targets." Richard said.

"Then I guess you need to get them out of the area. Send them to Chicago, or wherever, because as long as those two are down here they're going to be bait, and targets." Claudia was right, and Richard knew it. They looked over at Kenna, and Jared.

Kenna said. "I hate Chicago, I'm not going anywhere until this is over with. And I can take care of myself"

Everybody looked over at Jared. "What? I don't like Chicago either, and I feel that the safest place for me is beside Kenna."

Richard let out a little laugh. "Yeah, I can see that that is working for you."

"What? I'm not dead, am I?" Jared smiled back at him.

Richard asked. "So what are you, Mike? Are you FBI, or are you a city cop?"

Claudia answered the question. "He does some works for us. That's all that I'm saying, and I would like to keep it that way. Now that we know that Ronald is calling the shots, and maybe if we can keep one of his thugs alive, we might be able to get one of them to roll on him."

Richard looked over at Mike, saying. "Yesterday morning I sent two of my men, and our K- nine officer into the video store, and your wife didn't show up for work. Is there any connection there?"

"No." Mike yelled out in anger. "She was sick. What? Do you people think that she is tied up with this drug ring? And besides, they aren't operating out of the video store, anyways."

Richard stood there with a scolded look on his face. "Oh." Was all that he said.

"Look Mike, all that we are trying to do is go back to the places that Kenna and I were at, before this whole mess started." Jared pointed out to Mike.

Mike calmed down. "I understand that. But my wife isn't involved with drug trafficking. Do you understand that?"

"Yes I do. Sorry." Jared said.

"Now are you people done with me?" Mike asked.

Claudia spoke up. "Yes they are." She turned to Richard, saying. "If they have anymore question, I will be glad to answer them."

Mike walked over to the glass door, and looked outside before slowly opening the door. He then stuck his head out, and looked both directions. "What the hell are you doing Mike?" Clayton yelled out.

Startled, Mike jumped back into the room. "What did you do that for?"

"You look like you are trying to sneak out of here."

"I am. With all of the shooting that is going on, a man can't be too careful." Mike said, and then started to ease the door open again.

Kenna asked Claudia. "So are they operating out of Brett Harper's house, and was he involved?"

"I think the answers to that are. No, and no. Jeremy Black, and Brett were good friends, but I don't think that Brett was involved with the drugs. I mean as far as dealing them. Jeremy just hung out with Brett, because Brett always threw some wild parties. His house was always the spot for the college students to go to for parties. He was always getting busted, for the under aged drinking. But it's kind of funny, no charges ever stuck." Claudia explained.

James spoke up. "Yes, and that was because of his uncle Ben Miller. I guess he won't have to get him out of anymore trouble now."

"Oh yeah. How is that murder investigation going?" Claudia asked.

Richard answered. "It isn't. We've been a bit distracted, and now we're a person short."

"Are you not able to get anymore help?" Claudia asked.

"No. There isn't enough money, to send any help down here. This state is ran by a bunch of crooks out of Chicago, so they can care less what happens to us." James, who is a strong Republican said.

"Okay." Claudia said, with a surprised look on her face. "Sore subject I see."

Richard asked. "Are you people doing any kind of investigation, or are you just waiting for us to find everything for you?"

"No, we have an investigation on going. And yes you people have brought in some good evidence for us. Like the email that was on the three men that attacked your people at the morgue." When Claudia said this everyone tried to act like they didn't know about the email. "And don't act like you don't know what I'm talking about."

"So just who are you people after?" Richard asked.

"We would like to get Ronald Kindrick. That is the Ronald that they talk about on your recording. He is actually the boss, but nothing that we do leads us to him, and if we do catch him we don't have anything to arrest him on. In fact the closest thing that we have been able to get, that even remotely pointed to Ronald would be your recording. And that is pretty slim." Claudia explained.

Richard asked. "And what about the two guys that shot at us yesterday. Did you get anything off of them?"

Claudia looked down then looked back up at Richard. "No, not a thing. Well if you don't have anything else to ask me I'll be going." She looked around the room, and didn't get any response. "Okay then, it's been nice chatting with you." Claudia then walked out of the front door.

"The lying bitch." Came the response from Kenna. Everybody stared at her. "What? Don't tell me that you believe what she said, do you?"

James spoke up. "Well I don't now."

Richard asked. "What makes you think that she is lying?"

"By the way that she answered your questions. Most of the time she was either leaving out or covering up things that she said. For one thing, when you asked her about the guys that shot at us yesterday. She wasn't truthful with her answer. She said that they didn't find anything. I'm guessing that there was something in that car that she isn't telling us about." Kenna explained.

James said. "Richard. Kenna took courses in human behavior. You know, things like reading their body movements to tell rather they are being truthful or not."

"Oh. Okay, that explains it." Richard said.

Kenna asked. "Explains what?"

"Oh shit. I shouldn't have said that. It explains why you were so quiet." Richard figured that he had got himself into trouble with Kenna.

Her response was. "That's right. So now what are we going to do?"

"I don't know. We didn't get much to go on from those two, and we don't have any leads. And I don't think that we want to put you two out there as bait, to try and draw in the bad guys." Richard said. "We could go back and look at the videos from the video store."

Kenna kind of rolled her eyes, before saying. "Good luck with that. I believe I would rather go out driving around to see if we can get attacked."

"What's that suppose to mean?" Richard asked.

Kenna explained. "The only thing that I think that they were truthful about was that the video store isn't an outlet for selling drugs. But if you want to look at videos go ahead. Myself, I think I will make better use of my time."

"So what are you going to do?" Richard asked.

"I'm going to go talk to Katy Gomez again. Now that I know that Alison and Brett were a couple. I have some new questions to ask her." Kenna explained, and started to walk toward the door.

"Wait a minute." Richard said in order to stop Kenna. "I thought we decided to put the Alison Conner case on hold."

Kenna turned and walked back to face Richard. "Just what the hell do you expect me to do? Just sit around and wait. She wasn't telling me everything, and I plan to find out what she was withholding from me. Do you have anything else to add, if not I'm leaving?" She didn't wait for an answer. Instead she turned to Jared. "Are you coming?"

Jared answered. "Yeah, I believe I will." The two then walked out the door.

Once that they were gone Richard turned to face James, who was smiling, and nodding his head. "That is one scary woman."

"I know it, and she was such a little sweet heart when she was growing up." James said. "What happened to her?"

James answered. "Let's just say that she started fighting back, and taking care of herself. But that attitude, that's all Jenkins. She got that from her grandfather. Yeah John Jenkins is a mean old bastard."

Richard cringed, before saying. "Is, damn you mean that he is still alive?"

"Oh yes." James said, as he himself cringed. "He is alive, and well over by the river. Mae drags me over there at least once a month to see him."

CHAPTER XVII

Kenna and Jared walked up to Katy's apartment. Kenna knocked on the door, then stood back to wait on a response. Jared looked down at her wanting to say something, but she was too much in thought that he was afraid that if he said anything that she would just bite his head off. Kenna stepped forward, and knocked on the door a little bit harder.

"Who is it?" Came a voice from inside of the door.

"It's Kenna." That was all that she said, before the door opened up.

It was ten o'clock in the morning, and Katy opened the door with her bed clothes on. "I think that I might have over slept." Katy said.

Kenna pushed into the room, and headed straight to Katy's bedroom, then over to Alison's room. "I wanted to make sure that we were alone." She walked up to face Katy. "So how long have you two been doing drugs?"

Katy, with a surprised look on her face tried to shake her head, but Kenna was staring into her face making it hard to lie to her. "How do you know?"

Kenna closed in on her a little more. "I'm a cop. That's how I know, and I also know that Brett Harper was Alison's boyfriend. So just who is your boyfriend, Nathan Waters?"

Katy shifted side to side, before answering. "No. It's Cory Black, and he isn't like all the rest of those guys, he's a good guy. We would just do some pills together is all. He doesn't sell them or anything."

Kenna turned and faced Jared, then faced Katy again. "If he doesn't sell drugs, just what does he do then?"

Katy stood there blank faced. "I'm not sure."

"Well then let me fill you in. He's a drug dealer. Are you even still in school?"

Katy shifted side to side again, before answering. "Yes. Well I still have one class. It's at ten o'clock, so I probably need to be getting ready." She started to walk off to the bedroom.

"Katy, it's ten after ten right now. You have already missed your class." Kenna said.

"Oh. It is." Katy ran her fingers through her hair pulling her hair back off of her face. "I've probably flunked out of that class to now."

"Katy, you need to call your parents, and go back home." Kenna said to Katy, as she just stood there and looked around the room, and shook head. "Listen to me. If you keep this up, you're going to be dead, just like Alison."

"I can't go home. How am I going to tell my parents all of this? You know, how I flunked out of school and all. I can stay up here." She said, with a little smile as if she had come up with a great idea. "Cory will take care of me. He's coming over tonight. I can ask him tonight."

Kenna looked over at Jared trying to find a good way to tell Katy about her boyfriend. "No Katy you don't want to do that. You don't want to be mixed up with those people."

"No you don't understand, Cory isn't bad. Not like his brothers."

"Yes he was." Kenna let it slip, or maybe it was just her way of dropping a hint.

Now with a shocked look on her face, Katy said. "What do you mean, was? You say that like he is gone."

"Katy sit down, and let me explain."

"No you just tell me."

"Remember that night over at Jared's house." While Kenna was telling Katy, the tears started to form in Katy's eyes. "You know that I didn't have any choice. He shot at us first."

Katy turned around in a circle, while wiping the tears from her eyes. All that she really heard was that Kenna had killed her boyfriend. "You killed Cory?" She screamed out.

Kenna tried to explain. "He came there, because there is a hit out on Jared and me. That is what Cory done. He was a hit man."

"No your lying to me Cory is a good person." Katy wiped the tears from her eyes, and brushed her hair back again. Her mourning suddenly turned to anger. "You bitch, you killed Cory." She yelled out as she took a swing a Kenna. Kenna read her body motions right off. She blocked the punch that was coming at her, twisted Katy's arm to her back, and took her to the floor.

"Jared give me your cuffs. You're under an arrest for an attempted assault on a police officer." She said, as she put the restraints on the young lady. Kenna pulled Katy to her feet in order to escort her out of the building. "I suggest you now need to call your parents, to bail you out of jail. But if you don't want to, we can call them for you. Jared get the door."

The water works started to flow again, as she was being taken out of the building. "I can't call my parents. They're not going to understand. Oh my god, I can't believe that Cory is dead." Katy rambled on all the way to the car, and most of the way to the county police station.

Walking into the police station the three met up with James. "Whoa what's going on here?"

Kenna answered. "I'm arresting her for an attempted assault on a police officer." She didn't say any more, she just pushed on back to the nearest cell.

James looked to Jared for a more rational answer. "Kenna wants to send her home. The girl has been doing drugs, and has flunked out of college." Jared explained.

"Yeah and I killed her boyfriend, Cory Black, so she's not to happy about that. Just call her parents, and have them come and get her." Kenna smiled, and cocked her head a bit sideways. "Can you do that for me, Uncle Jimmy?"

"Ah, yeah I guess I can do that. So what are you two going to do?" James asked.

Kenna, who was heading out the door turned back to say. "I guess we'll go up to the state headquarters, and see if Richard has found out anything." She then proceeded out the door.

Once that they were out the door, Jared said. "Oh my god, you just manipulated him into calling Katy's parents for you."

"Yeah, so what's your point? You're not going to believe what that look, and little line has been able to get me over the years." Kenna thought for a few seconds. "Or was able to get my cousins and me out of."

"So you're saying your cousins would get youns into trouble, and you would have to get youns out of it?"

Kenna briefly hesitated, and then answered. "Not exactly, I might have helped us get into trouble." Her phone rang. She looked at the display, not recognizing the number she answered anyways. "Hello, this is Kenna."

"Hello Kenna. It's good to finely hear your voice."

"Who is this?" Kenna asked, while staring at Jared

"This is Nathan Waters."

Kenna looked around some what expecting to see him somewhere. "What do you want, and how did you get this number?"

"Let's just say that I might have picked up one of your business cards somewhere. And as for what I want. I just thought that I might just call you up, and chat a little bit. What's wrong with that?" Nathan asked.

Kenna's face went from a surprised look, because of Nathan calling her, to a pissed off look. "What's wrong with you wanting to chat? You son of a bitch, you're trying to have me killed."

"Oh, don't get mean with me. I'm not the one calling the shots."

"I know that." Kenna took another look around. "It's Ronald Kindrick, and you're just his boy, aren't you."

"Good one, but you're not going to get me roused all that easily. So why did you arrest Katy."

Kenna thought that he must be around here somewhere watching her. "How do you know that I arrested Katy? Did you see me haul her in?"

"Let's just say that I know things. Okay. You're not going to answer my question, are you?"

Kenna was still trying to think of ways to trip him up, but he was too smart for her. "Tell you what. I might tell you in person, you know face to face."

"No. I don't see that happening, besides you would probably just put a bullet in my head." Nathan said.

"No, I would just as soon arrest you. So why are you so interested in Katy, does she have some shit on you?"

"No, she's a sweet girl, just like your cousin was. By the way we didn't have anything to do with her death."

"I know you didn't. How did you know that she was my cousin?" Kenna asked.

"I've been asking around about you, Granddaughter to the legendary John Jenkins, and also a cousin to Jeffery Benson. Know wonder why they are having so much trouble getting rid of you."

"They. You're not including yourself in trying to get rid of me."

Nathan answered. "No, I'm telling you it's Ronald. Remember I'm just his boy. So what are you going to do stay here, and fight to the end?"

"You already know the answer to that question. Now what do you want?" Kenna asked again.

Nathan answered. "Ronald is coming into the area. He wants to know who is interrupting his drug flow, and why you are still alive."

Kenna asked. "Why are you telling me this?" It was too late he had already hung up the phone. "Damn it." Kenna said, as she took the phone away from her ear.

"Tell me that wasn't Nathan waters." Jared said.

"Yes it was."

"Well come on don't leave me hanging, what did he want?" Jared asked.

"He told me that Ronald is coming to the area. For some reason or another he warned me."

Jared looked at Kenna with a puzzled look on his face. "What did he do that for?"

Kenna answered. "I don't know. He didn't say. We need to get up to the state headquarters, and get with Richard." The two officers got into their borrowed police car, to go to the state office. "This thing is a piece of junk, Jared. Where did they borrow it from?"

"Oh, our friends over in Carmi loaned it to us." Jared explained.

Kenna thought for a few seconds, before asking. "Why would they loan a car to us?"

Jared smiled, and then said. "By the looks of it, they are probably hoping that we will total it out for them." The two continued on in silence to the state headquarters that is located twelve miles away from the county seat. Jared would glance over at Kenna on occasion, while she continued to look out the side window. "Thinking about Katy?"

Kenna turned to face Jared. "Yes, her too. What happened to those girls? I always thought that they had pretty good heads on their shoulders." She then turned to look back out of the window.

"I guess that they just got mixed up in the wrong crowd."

Kenna faced Jared again. "No, that's not the answer. You don't understand, that is not the way that they were brought up. They knew right from wrong. They knew not to be influenced by the wrong crowd. We're not talking about just some kids; we're talking about my cousin and her friend." She turned back to face out the window. It was almost as if she was blaming herself.

CHAPTER XVIII

They walked into the station, and went straight back to Richard's office. Even though he was on the phone, Kenna walked right in the room and sat down across from him at the desk.

"Well I'm going to let you go. Kenna and Jared are here." Richard said, while staring at Kenna, and hanging up the phone. "Do you need something?"

"Yeah, why. Were we interrupting you?" Kenna asked, as if she really cared.

"Yes you did."

"Yeah, whatever. It probably wasn't all that important. Who were you talking to?"

Richard shock his head, before saying. "Maybe it was confidential."

Kenna spoke up. "I doubt it. Who were you talking to?"

It was like Richard was cornered, with no way out but to tell her who he was talking to. "It was James, okay."

"What did he say about me?"

"He was telling me about Katy."

Kenna shifted her head from side to side, while saying. "And do you think that I was wrong."

With those brown eyes staring him down, if he said yes it was undetermined what his fate would be. "Your intentions were good, but I'm not to sure that it is going to work. Jimmy has called her parents, but I'm not to sure that we will be able to hold her until they get here."

"You just hold her as long as you can, then I will take care of her after that."

"And just how do you think that you will do that." While seeing the look on her face, Richard paused for a second, before saying. "Never mind. I don't think I really want to know. Do I?" Kenna shock her head. "Now what brings you in here?"

"Nathan Waters called me."

Richard turned slightly pale. "What did he call you for?"

"To warn me."

"To warn you?" Richard said. "Hell he's the son of a bitch that is trying to kill you."

Kenna replied. "He said that Ronald is the one that is after me, and he's coming down here."

The news just kept getting worse. "When, and what for?"

"Well, he wants me out of the picture, for one thing. He also wants to know why his drug shipments keep getting interrupted. And no I don't know when he is coming." Kenna explained.

"Interrupted, was that the way that he said it?"

"Yes interrupted. Why?" Kenna asked.

"Because it sounds to me like he might be getting his drugs back, with a slight delay."

Kenna added. "That would mean that Claudia is getting them back to him."

"Yes it does." Richard said. "I'm going to make a call, and I will need to ask you two to leave the room."

Upon Richard's request, the two left the room. Kenna turned to face Jared. She just stood there and faced him for a few seconds, and while she did, he stared into her eyes. It took all that he had to keep from binding down, and kissing her, or telling her that he loved her. "So, what are you thinking about?" She finally asked.

Well that didn't help things, and now he had to try to come up with an answer to why he was just staring at her. "I'm trying to read your thoughts." That seemed to be a good answer.

"Richard is thinking that the feds are giving Ronald his drugs back, doesn't he?"

That wasn't exactly what he was hoping that she was thinking about. "Yeah, I believe you are right. So, is Claudia dirty then?"

"I don't know, but I haven't trusted that woman yet." Kenna answered.

Richard had called Claudia. "Claudia, this is Richard."

"High Richard, what can I do for you?" Claudia asked.

"I have a source telling me that Ronald Kindrick is coming to our area. Have you heard anything about that?"

"No, not at all. Who is your source?" She asked.

"I'm not saying, but I also have reasons to believe that he has been getting his drugs back." Richard waited for a response back from Claudia, but there was a moment of silence on the other end of the phone.

"Are you trying to say that we are giving his drugs back to him?" She asked.

"Are they in lock up?"

"I'm going to send someone over to check. What else can you tell me about Ronald's visit to the area?" Claudia asked, and as if Ronald was just coming for a casual visit.

"Nothing really. I don't even know when he is going to be here." He could hear Claudia talking to someone in the back ground, so he paused for a little bit to listen in.

"You are right, the drugs are gone, and I have a suspect. He's one of my men, but would you bring him in for me?" Claudia asked. If things went bad, she didn't want to be the one to take out her own man.

"Yes I can do that for you. What is his name?"

"It's Tyler Cooper. You know him don't you?"

Richard was in a bit of a shock for a few seconds. "Yes I do. He's a hometown boy. I can't believe that he would go bad. I'm going to send Jared and Kenna after him. Do you know how I can find him?"

"Yes I do. He took the day off for a family thing. He should still be at home." Claudia gave out the information, and it pained her to have to do it.

Richard stepped out into the hallway to find Jared and Kenna. "Jared, Kenna. I need for you two to pick somebody up for me."

"Okay." Jared said, as he walked toward Richard for more instructions.

Richard hesitated for a few seconds, before saying the name. "It's Tyler Cooper."

Jared responded with a shocked look on his face. "Tyler Cooper, are you sure?"

"Yes, that is who Claudia told me. I couldn't believe it either." Richard said.

"Our daughters were best friends. They had sleep overs together. There must be some kind of a mistake. Are you sure that he isn't being set up?" Jared asked.

"I don't think so. It bothered her to tell me this. So please be discrete about it, this is why I am sending you." Richard turned, and walked back into his office.

Tyler Cooper just lived across town, which it's not a very big town, but it seemed like a long ride. Jared didn't say anything the whole trip, and Kenna didn't bring up any kind of conversation. "This is his house." Jared said, as they pulled into a driveway.

"Is that his car?" Kenna asked, as they were getting out of their car.

"Yes, and if he is here it looks like he might be alone." The two walked up to the front door. Jared knocked on the door, before yelling out. "Tyler, are you in there, it's me Jared Keppler." "Yeah, come on in the door is unlocked." Came the answer from inside of the house.

Jared reach down, turned the door handle, and Kenna eased the door open. "I'm coming in." Jared then said. The two walked in with their guns ready. Once inside the house, they could make out Tyler sitting at the kitchen table, with papers, pictures, and a gun sitting on the table. "What are you doing Tyler?"

"I know why you are here, and I can't let you take me to jail." He held up a picture. "Look what I found, it's Jenny and Katy. I took this one night when Katy was over. You know, Jenny cried herself to sleep every night for two weeks, after she lost her best friend. The whole time, I thought what I would do if my little girl were killed. I could see what you were going through, and I don't think that I could ever do that."

Jared spoke up. "It was hard. No father or husband should ever have to go through what I did. But why were you working for Ronald Kindrick?"

Tyler let out a little bit of a laugh. "Working with him, that's what you people think isn't it." Tyler held up a picture, and then yelled out. "Look what the son of a bitch sent to me." It was a picture of Tyler's wife and daughter. "It came with this note. We are watching your family, so you need to do what we tell you to do."

"Oh my god Tyler they threatened your family." Jared commented, as he holstered his gun. "Let's us just take you in."

Tyler cut him off. "You don't understand. I'm a dead man. The only thing that I can do now is protect my family."

Kenna spoke up. "They can do that, they can put them in protective custody."

"Yeah right. You don't even know who you are protecting them from. Do you really think you know who is involved? I know I sure didn't."

"We're going to get them." Jared said, with confidence.

"I wish I could believe you. Now here take this, and keep the picture of Katy, and Jenny for yourself." Jared took the pictures and papers, and as he was taking them, Tyler went for his gun. As he was picking up the gun, Kenna dove onto the table to try and get the gun.

At the time she was the only one that knew what he was going to do. Tyler being a very strong man took the gun to his head, with Kenna on his arm. He pulled the trigger blood, brain, and skull particles flew all over the wall and counter.

"What the hell Jared, didn't you see that coming?" Kenna yelled out, as she stood up.

"Oh my god no, I did not see that coming at all." Jared looked down at the papers that he was holding. "This is his suicide note."

"Yes. What the hell did you think that he was handing you, a confession. Didn't you hear him say that he was a dead man?" Kenna was shaking, and covered with blood as she said. "Well you're going to have to call Richard."

Jared took out his phone, and dialed Richard's number. "Richard, Tyler shot himself."

"Is there anybody else there?" Richard asked, while he was walking out the door.

"No just Kenna and I."

"Okay, make sure that nobody comes in that house."

Jared turned to Kenna. "Richard is on the way. He said for us to not let any one in."

"Well then I should probably go watch the front door." Kenna said

"Do you really think that is a good idea? You are covered with Tyler's blood." Jared pointed out to her.

"Your right. You should watch the front door."

Jared stood there at the front door looking out of the window. He couldn't help from thinking that this was partly his fault. He turned, and looked at Tyler's body lying on the floor, and thought that now he had lost two friends in two days. It was because of the drug ring, but he and Kenna were the ones that had stirred things up. He still held in his hands the pictures, and letters, and on top was the picture of Katy and Jenny. In a way he could almost understand why Tyler took his own life. Jared thought that he would take his own life for his wife and daughter to be alive.

Richard didn't waste any time getting there. "Jared are you okay?" Richard asked, as he walked into the house.

"Yeah I am alright. Here are some letters that he was writing when we came in." Jared handed Richard the stack of pictures, and papers.

"What's with the pictures?"

"Some of them he was just looking at, but there are also some that were sent, in order to threaten him into getting Ronald's drugs back." Jared explained.

Richard turned slightly pale, and mostly pissed. "They threatened harm on his family. These bastards won't stop at anything, will they?"

At that time Claudia walked into the house. "How did this happen, and why?" She asked in a tone that made it sound as if she were pointing blame on them.

Jared said. "He thought that it was the only way to protect his family."

"Besides, who told him that we were coming? You?" Kenna asked, while she was coming out of the study.

"I don't know what you are talking about."

"Bullshit. You called him, and told him that we were on our way here to pick him up, and take him in. Now didn't you?" Kenna yelled out at the federal officer.

"That's insane."

Kenna cut her off. "You mean stupid on your part. I checked his phone log, and you called him, probably right after you talked to Richard. Now didn't you?"

Claudia started to squirm, even before Richard asked. "Did you call him?"

"Yes, I called him right after I talked to you. But I was just checking on him to make sure that he was okay."

Kenna cut her off. "You lying bitch. He was getting things in order, because he knew that he was about to be arrested. Just who's life were you expecting for him to take? His or mine."

Everybody was quiet for a few seconds, while waiting for Claudia's answer. "I don't have to take this bullshit, Richard send me your report." She then stormed out of the door.

"Now what do we do?" Jared asked Richard.

"Well we won't be getting any help from her." Richard said.

"Well I hope you're not expecting an apology from me." Kenna calmly said.

"You two get out of here. I would say that the target on your back is getting larger." Richard told the two. "Oh, and Jared get out of that uniform. At least put on some jeans and a tee shirt. One of you two are going to have to drive your personal car."

The two officers looked at each other, before Kenna said. "Well I guess we are going to be riding around in a GMC pickup truck."

CHAPTER XIX

Jared's truck was back at the station, so they had to go back there to get it. The ride back was a quiet ride, the whole way Kenna just stared out of the window. Jared's mind was on his old friends Tyler, and Eddy.

"Do you think that there is any chance of getting these people?" Jared asked.

"Which people? If you're talking about Ronald; I do think that that might be possible, but I don't think that we have the resources to get any deeper into it." Jared didn't respond to Kenna's answer.

Back at the station Jared went to the locker room to change, while Kenna followed him in. "I'm going to change." Jared said.

"Yeah, I know. Oh I'm sorry, do you need some privacy?"

"Did you want to tell me something? I mean you were quiet the whole trip over here."

Kenna turned and faced the wall. "Is this better? I really didn't want to stand out there alone."

Jared changed his shirt, and started to pull his pants down. "Are you afraid to be alone?"

Kenna turned around to face the man with his pants down. "No I'm not afraid of anything. I just don't want to stand out there alone. Sorry." Kenna turned back around. "This whole mess has me confused. Who's in it, who's not, who we can trust, and who we can't. You got your damn pants on yet, I'm getting tired of staring at the wall?"

"Yes, you can turn around."

"Ronald has some contacts in this town. I say that we find them, so we can find Ronald. I mean really, the only thing we need to do is get rid of him, so that he would quit targeting us. Isn't that the way you see it?" Kenna asked.

Jared said. "This is my area. I think that we need to clean up the whole drug ring."

"Oh come on Jared. That isn't what I came down here for."

Jared started to walk pass Kenna to go out the door. "Did I hear a whine come out of you?"

Kenna grabbed his wrist, twisted it behind his back, and pushed him into the. "Now what you are about to do, is whine." She then proceeded to push his arm up to the middle of his back.

"Okay, okay. I got your point." Kenna then released his arm. "That hurt."

"And that is whining. Now get out so I can change clothes." Kenna said.

"Hey Jared, you off for the day." Jared turned to see Jackie Baker talking to him.

"No just changing clothes. Why, did you need something?" Jared asked.

"Raymond Perry has been looking for you. He said for me have you give him a call when you get back in. The number is on your desk that he wants for you to call him at." Jackie explained.

"Okay. Thank you Jackie." Jared picked up the phone to make the call.

"You're very welcome." Jackie said, with a flirtatious smile on her face.

"Raymond, this is Jared. Jackie said that you were looking for me."

"Yes. You back at the station?"

"Yes I am."

"Okay then, I will be there in about five minutes." Raymond said, before hanging up his phone.

"Raymond is on his way over to talk." Jared told Kenna when she came out of the locker room.

"Raymond Perry, the city cop?" Kenna asked.

"Yeah that's the one. I guess then we need to get out there and see what we can find out about Ronald's arrival." Jared said. A few minutes later a city squad car pulled up out front of the building. "There's Raymond".

Raymond walked into the office. "How are you doing Jared?"

"I'm doing okay. I'm assuming that you are talking about because of Tyler."

Raymond nodded his head. "What happened? Why would he do anything like that?"

"Are you talking about taking his life, or returning the drugs back to Ronald?" Jared asked.

"He was working for the drug ring? I can't believe that. He was always such a good cop."

"He was doing it under duress." Jared explained.

Puzzled, Raymond asked. "What do you mean?"

"They threatened his family. They had been following them, and taking pictures." Jared told Raymond.

"Well what are we going to do about it?" Raymond asked.

Kenna asked. "What do you mean we?"

"Look I had two friends. One was a state trouper, and the other was a fed. So I'm kind of taking this personally." Raymond explained.

Kenna said. "Well I don't know if you know it or not, but we now have a target on our backs?"

"Yes, I do know that. Look I done a tour in Iraq, so I know what it is like to be targeted. The people that we are up against are just a bunch of thugs, nothing professional about them. What we need is a combined police task force. That way we can go up against them, without any percussion against us." Raymond said.

"I think you have been watching too much television, Ray." Jared said. Richard walked into the building at that time.

"I don't know Jared. He may be on to something there." Raymond smiled, as he heard Kenna agree to his point.

"What is Raymond onto?" Richard asked.

Jared spoke up. "He wants to put together a task force to battle this drug ring."

"Okay then just who are we going to put on this task force?" Richard asked. "I'm a man short right now, and we're not going to get any help from the Feds now."

"I'm not too sure that they were helping us very much any ways." Kenna said. "Ronald is on his way here, and we really need to do something."

"Raymond how can you help us?" Richard asked.

"I have some connection. You might have to get me out of some trouble afterwards is all." Raymond said, with a smile on his face. Richard was shaking his head. "I'll admit it, when I was over in Iraq I was better then Gitmo. I can get us some answers, and I know where to start at."

Kenna said. "I like this plan."

"So what are you talking about? Are you wanting to go off and bang some heads together, and squeeze out some answers?" Richard asked.

"Yeah pretty much. Like I said, you might have to get me out of some trouble afterwards." Raymond answered.

"I don't know." Richard said.

"Yeah me either." Jared agreed.

"Oh come on you pussies. It sure beats the hell out of just driving around waiting to get shot at." Kenna yelled out.

"I'll probably regret this Raymond, but tell me what you have planned." Richard asked.

"Okay here is my idea. We go down to the C Club." Raymond looked straight at Kenna to say. "That is the one place to find all of the low lifes. Isn't that right Jared?"

Jared answered. "Yeah I might have heard that before."

"Okay whatever." Raymond continued on. "I'm sure that we can go down there, and all we have to do is walk into the place. There will be someone in there that will have information about Ronald. Now I don't have any problem going in there alone, but does anybody want to go with me?" He looked straight at Kenna as he asked.

"Oh yes, I'm definitely going." Kenna said.

"Well I guess you can count me in to." Jared added.

"Good now there's only one small problem. Richard can you talk to the chief for me?" Raymond asked.

"Yeah no problem." Richard and the chief went way back, so he wouldn't have any trouble talking to him.

"Okay good then I will go home, and get ready to go out." Raymond said with a smile on his face. "I'll meet you two back here in about thirty minutes."

CHAPTER XX

The three met up, and then took off for the bar. Jared drove his truck with Kenna as his passenger. Raymond went alone in his four while drive Ford pickup. As they rode along, Kenna asked. "So is this some sort of Red Neck bar".

Thinking for a few seconds, Jared then answered. "I don't think so. Why do you ask?"

"No special reason." Kenna answered. She was just hoping that the two men didn't stick out too much, because of the way that they were dressed, and the trucks that they drove. Moments later they pulled up in front of the C Club. Yeah they were definitely going to stick out. As soon as they walked into the bar Raymond walked up to a man at the bar, which had three women around him.

"Hey Jake, how's it going?" Raymond said to the man.

"What do you want Raymond?" The man asked.

"Just your undivided attention is all." Raymond said as he looked over the three young ladies. "Do your mothers know that you hang out with such a scum bag"?

"Go mingle." Jake told the young ladies, and then turned his attention back to Raymond. "Now what do you want"?

"I want you to tell me about Ronald Kindrick." Raymond explained.

"I don't think so." Jake said.

"It would be in your best interests to tell me." Raymond said.

"Or what? You don't think that you're going to…" Jake's sentence was interrupted by Raymond grabbing him by the hair on the back of his head, and slamming his forehead into the bar.

"Okay, we're going to get into trouble for this." Jared said.

With a smile on her face Kenna said. "No we're just having fun."

"You son of a bitch you can't be doing that." Jake told Raymond.

"Now back to my question. I would like for you to tell me about Ronald Kindrick." Raymond said as he put his hand on Jake's shoulder.

"Look if I say anything, I'm a dead man." Jake said.

Raymond dug his thumb into Jake's shoulder. "Don't try to play on my sympathies, because I really don't give a shit."

"I have friends." Jake yelled out.

Raymond looked around the room. "And yeah I see them rushing over to help you. Now talk." Raymond dug his thumb in even deeper.

"He's shacking up with some chick on Lincoln drive." Jake blurted out.

"Lincoln drive is a pretty long road. Can you narrow it down a little bit for us?" Raymond asked.

"No, that's all that I know."

"Then who is the chick?" Raymond asked.

"I think her name is Jamie Kirk." Jake explained.

"Okay then. Now that wasn't too painful was it? I'll tell you what we are going to do, we are going to find out where this Jamie Kirk lives, and head over to see her, so why don't you call your whores back over and enjoy the rest of the evening." Raymond patted Jake on the front of his shoulder, nodded to his partners, and then walked toward the door.

Kenna stopped him just before they reach the door. "Wait a minute. He's probably sending us into a trap."

"No Kenna we're already in the trap. The call has been made, and Ronald's people are already in place." Raymond answered Kenna's question then said to Jared in a loud voice. "Let's drink to fallen friends before we go." Raymond lowered his voice as he spoke to Kenna. "Can you hold your liquor?"

"Better then my partners. I am a Jenkins you know."

Raymond smiled at Kenna. "Sounds like a challenge then, bartender three lights." The bartender set the drinks on the bar. As he was reaching for them Raymond said in a loud voice, while looking down the bar. "My friend Jake is buying these for us."

The bartender looked down the bar at Jake, who nodded his head in approval.

Raymond raised his bottle while saying. "Here's to our fallen friends, and Illinois corn." The three tipped they're bottles up, and Raymond and Kenna's bottles came back down on the bar empty. Raymond looked down the bar at Jake. "Hey bartender another round." The bartender looked down at Jake, and Jake nodded in approval.

"And what is the reason for this?" Kenna asked.

Raymond tipped his bottle toward Jake before taking a drink. "See the guy that just walked in the back door? He's letting Jake know that the guns are in place. Now just follow my lead." Raymond walked to the end of the bar where Jake was sitting. "Who's your friend Jake?"

Jake took a deep breath and let out a sigh. "He's nobody." Jake turned toward the man. "And this is one of our local cops."

"That's right. So do you have a name, or do you want us to just call you Jakes scum bag friend?" Raymond asked the man.

He responded with saying. "The name's Derek. Now why are you harassing us?"

"Harassing. Is that what you think is going on here? We're just having a friendly little chat here. Hell Jake why don't you buy us another round of drinks?" Raymond turned his attention back to Derek. "You see Jake here is loaded, he makes money by selling drugs to kids. Do you sell drugs to?"

Derek answered. "No."

"So what do you for a living then? Are you a hit man for Ronald Kindrick?" Raymond boldly asked.

Derek looked at Jake then back at Raymond before answering. "No."

"Oh come on Derek you can tell me. The three of us are cops. Jake tell him what you do." Raymond turned to Jake for his answer.

Jake said. "I sell drugs."

Raymond smiled and slapped Jake on the back. "There we go. Now it's your turn Derek. What is your occupation? Hey bartender, Jake wants to buy us all a round of drinks. Beers for the cops. What are you drinking Jake?"

"Rum and coke." Was Jake's answer.

"Rum and coke for the drug pusher and you probably need to start the big shot want to be off with something light and fruity. Is that right Derek?" Raymond asked. All he was trying to do now was intimidate Derek.

"I'll have a rum and coke." Derek told the bartender then turned to face Raymond. "And you are the big shot want to be."

"Oww that hurt." Raymond said, and then turned to his fellow officers laughing. "You see Derek, this badge and this big gun make me a big shot. Do you have either one?"

Kenna could tell because of his body movements that he had a gun but not a badge. She picked up her beer and took one drink from it. "I think he is packing an illegal weapon." Kenna casually said.

When she said that Derek had a stupid attack come over him. He actually went for the weapon that was tucked into the small of his back. Kenna spun toward him, taking her beer, and smashing it into the bridge of Derek's nose. Derek went straight down to his knees, while blood and beer poured out onto the floor. Kenna took the last drink from her beer and then said. "Damn spilled a good beer."

Raymond asked Derek. "Did that hurt as bad as it looked like it did?" Raymond picked up the gun and Derek. "I think you have some explaining to do here." Raymond picked up the towel that the bartender laid on the bar for the bloody man. He put it in Derek's face, and grabbed his nose while doing it.

"Oww you son of a bitch that hurts." Derek said.

"Just trying to stop the bleeding. You weren't going to shoot us were you?" Raymond asked.

Derek said. "You will not make it outside of this bar alive."

"Shut up Derek." Jake said.

After Derek pulled out the gun people started filing out of the building, until the only people left were the three officers, Jake, Derek, and the bartender.

Kenna looked back at the bartender, who said. "I'll be hiding back here." As soon as he said that Kenna drew her forty five. The front door and the back door opened at the same time. Raymond pulled Derek around in front of him, as he turned to face the front door, with Derek's gun drawn. Kenna took aim at the back door, as two men with automatic pistols entered shooting sporadically without bullets coming close to any target. Kenna squeezed off two shots, taking down both men. She then turned toward the front door, where there were two more men with slightly better aim. They had shot a number of times one shot hit Jake, who was trying to get away. The three officers fired off a total of twelve shots at the two men. As those two men went down, so did Derek.

Kenna looked over at Raymond asking. "Is he dead?"

Raymond answered. "No our tough guy just fainted is all. What about you Jake are you still alive?"

Jake answered in a faint voice. "Just barely I'm loosing a lot of blood."

Raymond walked over to Jake while Kenna went to check the back door, and Jared the front door. "Where did you get shot at?"

"My leg. Can't you see it?" Jake yelled out.

"Hell Jake it barely grazed you." When Raymond said that, Jake raised up to look at his leg. His jeans had a hole in them, but his leg didn't.

In embarrassment Jake said. "Okay I'll be alright."

"How many more are there?" Raymond asked. Kenna locked the back door, checked the two gunmen, and walked back over to the center of the club.

"I don't know. I didn't even know that these people were going to show up. What kind of shit did you bring down on me?"

"Like I told you earlier we're looking for Ronald Kindrick. That is the kind of shit that is coming down." Raymond answered him. Outside red lights were starting to show up.

"My answer is still the same. All I am is a dealer." Jake laughed a little bit before saying. "Looks to me like you have killed off anybody that might be able to give you any answers."

"This is the police. We have the place surrounded." Came a voice from outside.

Jared yelled back at them. "This is Jared Keppler it is safe for you to come in."

"Jared this is Richard we're coming in." Richard and Clayton walked into the building. "Well how is the intel gathering going?"

Raymond said. "Not so well this guy isn't talking, that guy collapsed under the pressure, and I'm guessing that those four guys are our best sources."

"Yeah probably are." Richard said right before the door opened up, in walked three city patrolman, and the chief of the city police.

"What the hell is going on here Richard?" The Chief Ed Miller asked.

"Well as you can see we've had a little bit of a shoot out." Richard answered.

"Yes that I can see. Now tell me why there has been a shoot out in my town. And who are these people, are they on your force?" Ed asked.

"Well you know Jared."

"Yes I know Jared. And I also know Raymond who is out of his jurisdiction, so who is this young lady?"

Richard answered. "This is Kenna Jenkins; she is out of the main office in Springfield."

"Jenkins huh. Any relation to that old bastard over by the river?" Ed asked Kenna, while he was extending his hand out to her.

Kenna shook his hand while she answered. "Yeah the old bastard is my grandfather."

Ed quickly lost a smile that was on his face. "I'm sorry."

"For what?" Kenna asked. "For calling him an old bastard or that he is my grandfather? Either way it's alright. And what about you any relation to the prosecutor."

"No not at all." Ed answered Kenna's question and then turned back to Richard. "Now why has there been another shoot out in my city involving your people?"

"They were just in here asking some questions and there was an apparent ambush on them." Richard explained.

"Questions about what?"

"Questions about Ronald Kindrick." Ed perked up when he heard the name. "Heard of him have you?"

Ed answered. "Yes I have nice gentleman."

Shocked by Ed's answer Richard asked. "Are you serious, nice gentleman?"

"No I'm being sarcastic. Why are you in here asking about him for?"

Richard answered. "Because we believe that he is in the area."

"In my town. What is he doing in my town?"

Kenna answered. "He is here to kill me."

"You, what did you do to piss him off?" Ed asked Kenna

"I have been interrupting his drug trafficking and killing off his people, and apparently some that he liked."

Mike Davis, one of the officers that had came in with Ed, and who had been quietly standing back spoke up. "She killed off two of his nephews."

"Holey shit." Jake blurted out, and caught everyone's attention. "No wonder why he is pissed at you."

"Huh, killing off mob family, this could be interesting." Ed remarked thought for a second then said. "You know, I think that I would like to stay close to this action while you are in town. For me it gets a little boring around here. What about you Mike care to hang with them for a little bit."

"Well I would rather not, those two attract lead." Was Mike's answer.

"Yes I can see that, but I don't see anything wrong with having a little bit of lead flying over my head. So do we have any leads on our Mr. Kindrick?" Ed asked.

Raymond answered. "The only thing that we have been able to get is that he is shacked up with a Jamie Kirk on Lincoln drive."

Ed turned to one of his officers. "Tony run that name and address for me."

"That isn't necessary. She's at 11 hundred North Oakland avenue has been for about a week now. I think your buddy dug that name out of the obituaries." Tony said.

Everyone looked over at Jake, who was now trying to find a way to squirm out of the information that he had given up. "She used to be his girlfriend."

"Oh this is great." Kenna said. "We're about as close to getting Ronald as we were when we walked into this place." Kenna walked up to Jake, stared him right in the eyes, and said. "He did mention Lincoln. Tony did Jamie even live anywhere on that street?"

"Not unless there is some government housing there, because that is all she ever lived in along with her three children." Tony explained.

Kenna didn't stop staring at Jake the whole time that she was talking. "Did you sell that woman the drugs that made those children orphans?"

Jake turned his head slightly trying to escape Kenna's glare. "I don't know Tony's right I read her name in the obituaries."

"No you didn't you know her, and you also know of something on Lincoln Drive. What is on Lincoln drive that you're not telling us about?" Kenna asked.

Jake yelled out. "Nothing. I don't know of anything on Lincoln Drive."

"Would somebody mind getting this man out of here?" Kenna asked.

Tony grabbed him by the arm to escort him out of the building. "Should I put him under arrest?"

"For what?" Kenna asked. "For giving us information that is leading to the arrest of a major drug dealer? No you need to put him back on the street."

"Wait a minute here I didn't say anything. You're trying to set me up to get killed aren't you?" Jake yelled out while Tony was grabbing his arm.

Tony looked over at Kenna who then said. "Get him out of here Tony."

Kenna walked over to Derek who was still lying on the floor. She grabbed his shirt with her left hand, and slapped him with her right hand. When Derek's eyes popped open Kenna said. "You play dead pretty good, but you weren't fooling me. Now get up here so we can talk." Kenna helped stand the man up. "You know that you are a dead man now don't you?"

"What are you talking about?" Derek asked while he was trying to look around.

Kenna explained. "Your acting skills suck you have been lying there on the floor listening to everything that has been going on, now haven't you?"

"No ah, no I ah, I was out I think some body hit me." Derek was able to spit out.

"Well okay then, I guess we will send you out in the street with Jake then." Kenna said as she was releasing his shirt. "Good luck out there, now you do know the first one back to Ronald with the correct information is going to live, don't you?"

"Okay." The idiot said, and then started to run towards the door.

"Stop him." Kenna said with a bit of annoyance in her voice. Mike Davis quickly stuck out a huge arm, clothes lining the man, and sending him to the floor. Kenna walked over and looked down at the man. "Were you born stupid, or has your brain been fried by too many drugs?"

Derek looked up at Kenna in confusion. "What are you talking about?"

"You know where Ronald is at, and you are getting ready to run back to him. Little news flash, that is the man that we are after. So if you don't mind just go ahead and tell us where we can find him." Kenna explained to the man on the floor.

Derek lie there for a few seconds realizing that he had just screwed up. "So you ah, ah you think I know where he is at don't you?"

Kenna answered. "Yeah you kind of give it away when you started to run out the door."

"You're right I am a dead man Ronald's people are going to find me and kill me." Derek said before wiping his hands down over his face. "I'm having a shitty day."

"You do know that you run a better chance of surviving if we get Ronald don't you?" Kenna asked.

"I don't think it would help me any, but I'll tell you anyways. You know those storage buildings on North Illinois Avenue?"

Kenna looked up at Mike, who said. "Yeah I know where they are at."

"So do I." Jared said. "The day that we were shot at in front of Brett Harper's house we went right by there. And you know I did kind of slow down a little bit when we went past there."

"I'll be damned." Richard said. "So that is why they have been after you two, they think that you saw something don't they?"

Derek stood up. "You did see something. There was a big shipment that came in that day."

Mike let out a laugh, and every body turned to look at him. "And of course we drove by there a couple of days ago on our little ride. I'm sure it looks like to them that you are watching the place."

"Well I'm thinking that we need to check out this place again." Ed said, and then turned his attention to Richard. "What do you think; get on it while the trail is still warm?"

Richard replied back. "I'm guessing that would be a good idea seeing how that we have city backing right now. So are we calling this a joint effort?"

"Yeah sure." Ed answered. "What about the Feds, are we going to get them in on it?"

Richard thought for a second. "I don't know of any Feds that I trust, do you?"

Ed didn't hesitate before saying. "No not at all. Let's mount up."

Once outside they saw Derek still pleading for his life. "Jeffery you and Amanda take these two in and lock them up." Ed yelled out to two young officers.

Amanda asked. "Do you want us to charge them?"

"No just put them in a holding cell, I'll deal with them when I get in." Ed answered. The two rookies, who have just joined the force a month earlier cuffed the two, and escorted them to they're car. As Ed watched them leave he said. "They're a couple of nice kids; it will be good to keep them out of the way. Well let's do this."

CHAPTER XXI

Everybody loaded up to head to the location that Derek told them about. Ed led the pursuit followed by his men. Even though this had started out to be Richards bust he held a second place. Most likely it was because he had already lost one man, so now his confidence to lead was down. The storage lot only had one way in, so it wasn't hard to close off any exits. Ed took in three cars with two officers per car. There were two sets of buildings set parallel to each other. There weren't any cars around to indicate that there was anybody there. Ed drove down between the buildings with his other two cars on the outside. Richard took the middle as well stopping at the front, while Kenna and Jared went to the right and Raymond to the left.

"What are you thinking Richard?" Ed asked over the radio.

Richard answered. "Honestly I'm thinking bad Intel. What about you do you think that there is anything here?" No sooner did Richard say this that two men stepped out of a walk in door of the building to Richards left, and started shooting at both Richard's car and Ed's car.

Hearing the shots Kenna got out of Jared's truck, and ran around the building. When she rounded the corner she fired off five shots, forcing the two men back into the building. "Richard are you okay?" Kenna asked.

"Yes I'm fine." He answered Kenna then turned to Clayton who was in the passenger's seat. "How about you Clayton?"

"Yeah I'm fine let's get them." Clayton said while exiting the car. Jared and Raymond joined up with the other three.

"Ed are you guys okay?" Richard radioed to the city officer.

"Yeah we're fine." Ed answered while his other four officers joined up with him.

"Did you hear a car start up?" Clayton said just before the sounds of crashing metal came from the other side of the building.

"What the hell?" Richard said, but Kenna didn't waste any time, she quickly ran to the other side of the building, with Raymond and Jared following behind her. On the other side they saw three SUVs heading off into a corn field.

"The sons of bitches are getting away." Kenna said, before heading back toward the cars. "Come on Jared we have to go."

"Wait a minute you can't just go chasing off after them." Richard said to Kenna.

Kenna stopped briefly to say. "Richard you're joking we can't just let them get away now.'

"We are out manned, and we just escaped one of their traps and you want us to jump into another one?" By now you could see a lot more fear in Richard's eyes.

Kenna walked within two steps of him to say. "Are you going to puss out on me now? The only way to stop all of this shit just took off through that corn field and you just want to sit back and let them go. Are you two with me?" Kenna said to Jared and Raymond without turning around, or taking her eyes off of Richard.

Richard said with a crack in his voice. "I can't allow Jared to go."

"Raymond you don't work for this gutless bastard are you with me or not?"

"Hell yeah let's go." Raymond answered.

Kenna started backing away eyeing Richard the whole time. "She'll get you killed. Her partners don't stand much of a chance with her." Kenna started back toward Richard by the look on her face everybody knew what was about to happen.

"Kenna please don't just let it go." Jared said as he stepped between the two. "Come on I'll drive you."

"I'm ordering you not to go with her." Richard said.

"I know, but I said that I was going to stay with her until this was over with and I'm going to no matter what." Jared said.

Clayton said to Raymond. "I guess that I'm riding with you then."

"Hey what are you people getting ready to do." Ed asked.

Richard answered. "We're discussing it now. What about you?"

Ed answered Richards Question. "I have two men going into the building right now to check it out."

Everyone stared at each other wide eyed right before Richard said back to Ed. "I would suggest that you not let them go in there." It was too late there was a light explosion with a lot of flames. "You people need to get going if you're going to catch these bastards."

As the four left they could hear Ed on the radio trying to get a response from the two men that he had sent into the building. Jared looked at Kenna before pulling out onto the highway. "They're dead, aren't they?"

Kenna responded. "I'm afraid that they are. Now watch close because I don't think that our bad guys are too far away. They would want to watch to make sure that their building burnt up. I'm not seeing where they came out of the corn at." Raymond was close behind them when suddenly behind them three SUVs busted out of the corn field onto the highway, and headed the opposite direction. Kenna yelled out. "They're behind us.

"Hang on." Jared said as he done a U-turn in the middle of the road. As he turned around Raymond barely missing them past by, and then also did a U-turn.

Kenna grabbed onto anything that she could find. "Oh and I am going to get you guys killed."

Jared glanced over at Kenna with a puzzled look on her face. "What? Well you were right they were waiting around to make sure that the building burnt."

As they were reaching speeds of over one hundred miles an hour Kenna, who was still hanging on for her life asked. "So what are we going to do when we catch up to them."

Jared smiled and nodded his head. "That is what the reinforced bumper and brush guard is for." By now they were just about twenty yards behind the last car. Kenna braced herself as Jared ran his pickup truck into the back end of the SUV. As he hit the car he turned the wheel slightly to the right to send the car into a tail spin. The SUV went into a tail spin, but also his truck done a U-turn at ninety miles per hour. With the SUV now going down the highway sideways, and Jared's truck going backward he rammed the car causing it to start flipping over sideways. Jared locked up the breaks making the truck come to a stop right before the car quit rolling. Looking over at Kenna he nodded, and smiled. "Yeah, ah huh what did you think of that?"

"Son of a bitch you could have killed us." Kenna said while she pulled on the door handle to get out of the truck. "What the hell is the matter with this door?"

Jared reached over to unlock Kenna's door. "What do you mean? Don't you think that was a text book stop?"

Kenna made another attempt to open the door this time with success. "Textbook my ass you got lucky." Kenna said while jumping from the truck, and pulling out her forty five.

Raymond and Clayton pulled up beside the two officers. "You two okay?" Clayton asked.

"Yes stay on those other two cars." Kenna yelled out. She walked up to the SUV with her gun ready, but it was unnecessary, because there were two dead occupants inside of the car. Kenna looked back down the road to see red and blue lights coming at them. "Who is that?"

Jared called out on his radio. "Who is coming up on this scene?"

The answer came back. "It's Tony."

"There are two men dead in this car. Can you secure the scene so we can get back into the pursuit?" Kenna asked over her radio.

"Yes go ahead get the rest of those bastards." Tony radioed back. While the two officers were getting back into the truck, Tony added. "We lost two officers back at the warehouse."

"I'm sorry." Kenna said as she sat down in the truck. Jared quickly made a U-turn in the middle of the road and headed back after the other two cars. "Where are youns Clayton?" Kenna asked over the radio.

"Still heading north on fifty one." Clayton answered.

Richard came on the radio. "We have county blocking the road south of De Soto."

Clayton quickly responded back. "Yeah ten four we're all stopping." County had placed two semi-trucks in the middle of the road ahead. They were standing beside two squad cars that were parked on the shoulder, with two county officers on each side. The SUVs stopped within fifty yards of the road block, and the two officers in the truck stopped forty yards behind them. "Are we in a good place?" Clayton asked Raymond.

"No, I don't think so." Raymond said, before putting his truck in reverse to back out. The back door of the second SUV opened up, and a man with an automatic rifle started shooting at them. All that the two men could do was duck down into the floor board, as the bullets went through the windshield and engine killing the engine.

Jared and Kenna pulled up within five feet of Raymond's truck. As soon as they were stopped Kenna opened the door, and dove for the ditch with a forty five in each hand and ammunition bag on her shoulder. As soon as she hit the ditch she started firing off rounds at the man with the rifle. The man stopped firing long enough to where Clayton and Raymond could exit the truck. Two things that you don't do in southern Illinois are kicking a man's dog, or damage his pickup truck. Raymond stepped out of his truck with his Mossberg five hundred tactical shot gun.

"You sons of bitches." Raymond yelled out as he started firing off shots and walking toward the two SUVs. Raymond must have grabbed an assortment of turkey, goose, or small game loads, but whatever he was shooting was destroying the car. This gave the other three officers a chance to get in line with Raymond. With their guns drawn they hurried toward the SUVs.

"Stick your hands out of the windows now." James Benton yelled out over a loud speaker. The two men in the back car weren't going to respond, and the men in the lead car thought that this might be a good time to make a getaway. They turned to go over the shoulder, but as soon as they did Kenna shot out both right tires. This made the car spin its wheels in the ditch. The two men jumped from the car to attempt an escape on foot. The passenger took a shot while he was jumping from the car, and Kenna quickly returned fire dropping the man instantly.

"Don't shoot." The driver yelled out as he exited the car.

"Put your hands on your head and get on your knees." James yelled back at him. "If there is anybody else in the car you need to get out now." The back passenger door opened up and a man in his late forties showed himself. "Put your hands on your head." James yelled out at the man, but the arrogant man stepped out of the car with his hands down to his side.

"You heard him Ronald hands on your head." Kenna said to the man while she had her forty five aimed at his chest hoping to pull the trigger.

"Are you the bitch that killed my two nephews?" Ronald asked.

Kenna answered as she took careful aim at the man. "Yes I'm that bitch."

"I came here because I sent a lot of good men to get you. Well they all failed, so I had to ask myself if they were really good men or if you were just that good." Ronald explained.

"Yeah and what did you decide?"

"I decided that I should have just left you alone." Ronald said as he put his hands on top of his head. Jared moved in behind the man, patted him down, and removed a hand gun from the small of his back. After doing so he then pulled Ronald's hands down to cuff him.

"Come on Ronald we have a car waiting on you." Jared said as he started to lead the man away. "We got him Kenna."

"Yeah I guess it's over now." Kenna looked back down the road to see several more police cars coming down the road. She holstered her guns and walked over to James Benton. "I'm ready to get out of here Uncle Jimmy, do you have someone that can take me back to my car?"

"Yes I do. Gregg can you take Kenna back to her car? You look tired why don't you go back to my house and get some sleep." James said as Kenna was getting into county squad car.

"I plan to." Kenna sat quietly on the ride back to the State Headquarters. "Thanks for the ride." She told Gregg as she was getting out of the car.

"Are you going to be okay?" Gregg asked.

"Yeah I'll be okay." Kenna walked over to her car, while watching Gregg pull away she reach for the door handle. When she started to tug on the handle her phone rang. She pulled it out of her pocket and looked at the display, which read unknown caller. "Hello."

"Hello Kenna thought I might just call you up and thank you for helping me get a promotion."

Right away Kenna knew who it was. "Nathan Waters. I guess we will be gunning for each other now, won't we?"

"Why would I come after you after all that you have done for me?" Nathan asked.

"So you're saying that I am going to have to hunt you down?"

Nathan let out a little laugh before answering. "I'm not sticking around here winter is coming on and it gets nasty around these parts. Besides the laws are too strict and you people are too set on enforcing them. So I am hoping that this is good bye."

"This is goodbye as long as you stay away." Nathan hung up before she got the words out. "Damnit." Kenna said as she hung up her phone. Her hand was shaking as she reached for the door handle again. She knew that he was watching her from somewhere and she didn't like the thought of being stocked and bullied. She took a deep breath before opening the car door. She looked in the back seat before sitting down in the car. Nervously she put the key into the ignition, started the car, put it in gear, and drove off. Once that she was a couple miles down the road and the car didn't blow up she started to feel relieved.

CHAPTER XXII

The next day Kenna walked into the State Headquarters about ten o'clock in the morning. The first person that she saw was Richard. "Good morning." He said to the young lady.

"Good morning. You seem rather happy this morning." Kenna said with a smile on her face.

"I am. We made a pretty good bust last night, and now things can get back to a little more normal around here." Richard explained.

Still smiling Kenna said. "Yes, and I can get back to what I came down here for."

"No that is another thing that makes this a good morning. I have orders here for you to go to Belleville and report to Don Cox. He's the supervisor in that area."

Kenna's smile quickly faded away to be replaced with a look of anger she leaned forward saying. "What the hell did you do?"

Richard lost his smile to be replaced with a look of fear. "Whoa wait a minute I didn't have anything to do with it. Here are the orders they came in at eight o'clock this morning and I just got here myself."

Kenna took the orders, read them over, and went off alone to make a phone call. The orders came from her supervisor in Springfield, so there was no getting out of it. After hanging up her phone she said to Richard. "I guess I'm going to Belleville." She then turned and walked out the door.

"Hey what's up?" Jared who was just outside the door asked.

Without stopping Kenna answered. "I'm leaving."

"Wait a minute what do you mean leaving."

Kenna stopped and turned around to answer Jared. "I have orders to report to the Belleville office."

"So this is it huh just leave you weren't even going to say goodbye?" Jared asked.

Still pissed about the orders Kenna was also starting to get irritated. "What are you expecting? Goodbye, isn't that good enough?"

Jared moved a little closer to her before answering. "No it's not. I can't just let you walk out of my life like this. I'm in love with you, and I want to be with you. I've been in love with you from the first time that I met you." While he was pouring out his heart Kenna looked down at the ground. "Well do you have anything to say?" Jared smiled while waiting on his answer.

Kenna looked up at Jared. She looked into his eyes for a few seconds then replied. "Jared. I can't deal with this shit right now." Jared stood there with his heart ripped out as Kenna got into her car and drove away out of his life. Once she was down the road a ways she looked at the hat that she had taken of Jared's then took a deep breath while placing her hand on the hat.

THE END

www.ingramcontent.com/pod-product-compliance
Lightning Source LLC
LaVergne TN
LVHW041949070526
838199LV00051BA/2959